THE SECRET
TRAIL

ALSO BY ANTHONY ARMSTRONG

The Trail of Fear (1927)
The Trail of the Lotto (1929)
The Trail of the Black King (1931)
The Poison Trail (1932)

Other Books

Lure of the Past (1920)
The Love of Prince Raameses (1921)
Wine of Death (1925)
Patrick, Undergraduate (1926)
Apple and Percival (1931)
Britisher on Broadway (1932)
Easy Warriors, Etc. (1932)
Ten Minute Alibi (1934)
Without Witness (1934)
Cottage into House (1936)
The Pack of Pieces (1942)
The End of the Road (1943)
When the Bells Rang (1943)
No Higher Mountain (1951)
He Was Found in the Road (1952)
Spies in Amber (1956)
The Strange Case of Mr Pelham (1957)
One Jump Ahead (1973)

THE SECRET TRAIL

ANTHONY ARMSTRONG

A Jimmy Rezaire Story

WILDSIDE PRESS

Published by Wildside Press LLC.
www.wildsidepress.com

CHAPTER I

JIMMIE COMES OUT

Jimmie Rezaire sat on a seat in St. James' Park, London, and expanded his lungs to their full extent, drawing in gulps of the cool October air. Small and well-made with a sharp-featured face and restless bright eyes, he seemed to relax himself with the abandon of a man who has just thrown off a heavy burden.

And undoubtedly he had. For he was free at last. That very morning he had been released from prison after serving his sentence—reduced to some extent for exemplary behavior, and for a little matter of helping a warder. Once behind the bars, Jimmie had not indulged in any vindictive foolishness or wild attempts at escape; his one idea had been to get out again as quickly as possible by legitimate methods. Once out, he was more than half determined to pit his brains once again against those of the police force; for the name of Jimmie Rezaire was well known in the upper strata of the underworld, and was even mentioned with admiration since the "job" for which he had done time. Jimmie laughed derisively as he recalled the Prison Governor's parting words about running straight and using his undoubted brains for the community instead of against it. And even the Governor had laughed when, on expressing a hope that they would not meet again, Jimmie had countered that their first introduction had been forced on him against his wish.

He recalled with almost a feeling of pride how nearly, after all, he had escaped capture,—that midnight chase across London, the fight with the police in the flat, the dash in the stolen car through Hampshire, those breathless final moments at Beaulieu. At the last, safety had been in his fingers and he had let it slip because with it went an encounter with his revengeful partner, Long Sam, whom some hours earlier he had attempted unsuccessfully to betray. Sam had escaped that night, doubtless breathing vindictive hatred—but Jimmie himself had been taken. Thank God no murder had been proved against him; as far as he knew he had been guiltless of that.

Well, well—he again took lungfuls of the free air of London—he was clear of everything now; and Long Sam, so he had heard, was in

America and likely to stay there, with the warrants out against him here. In the meantime he was free—free to take up whatever money-making line of business he liked, illicit or not. He thought of the police and laughed shortly. He did not give a snap of the fingers for all the brains of the police force. He had fooled them before and he could do it again if he wanted. The only reason they had got him that time was that he preferred capture to escape in Sam's company.

His eye roving round fell upon a weedy little man in a bowler who had been walking up and down the path in front ever since he had sat down. Jimmie Rezaire had never seen him before that morning, but he was still waiting for the other to speak to him. For the weedy man had been outside the prison gates when he had been released and had been casually reappearing ever since. At first Jimmie had taken him to be a police-spy; then he had wondered with a little catch of the breath if he was a friend of Sam's; finally he decided it was some blackmailing jackal of the underworld who wanted a share in the money which Jimmie was known to have put secretly away before being caught. After this decision, he ignored the fellow, not even bothering to shake him off; for he knew well how to deal with that class.

At last the weedy loafer casually sat down beside him and began ostentatiously to read an evening paper.

"Well?" said Jimmie abruptly.

The other started; then said: "I wondered if you'd noticed me."

"Notice!" laughed Rezaire scornfully. "Do you think I'm blind? Well, what do you want? Money?"

"I allus want money. But not this time. I'm acting *for* someone. Some bloke as'ud like to get in *touch* with you. Mutual benefit, sez the bloke. That's why I trailed on when you came out. There was I, a-waiting at the gate," he concluded humorously.

Jimmie was slightly interested. This was unexpected. "Who is it?" he asked.

"A big bloke. Big job—with lots o' dough in it, 'e sez. If you're interested you're to ring Park 8465 after seven-thirty tonight and ask for Mr. Jack."

"Who is it?" repeated Rezaire.

"That's all I was to say," said the other, getting up. "Can't get no more outer me. Park 8465. Good day, mister."

He shuffled off and was gone, leaving Rezaire smiling disdainfully. It was of course quite clear to him that some gang or other wanted him to join up with them. Talent in any profession was always sought after. He was not over-modest and he knew that he was a really clever criminal.

He knew too that his exploits in that astounding flight from the police had echoed through England for many days.

He wondered vaguely what sort of gang it was. Ring Park 8465. Someone big judging by their careful methods. Probably forgery or a big jewel job, he decided. Then he dismissed the matter from his mind, for he was not really interested. Apart from the fact that he infinitely preferred to work by himself or to choose his own helpers, he was not in need of money at the moment. He had a tidy little sum, the proceeds of that last big coup, tucked away in a Paris bank under a name which only he knew.

He got up and walked thoughtfully to the Grand Cross Hotel near Trafalgar Square where he had taken a room on the top floor. Jimmie Rezaire always believed in effacing himself and held that a small room in a big London hotel was about the best hiding place possible.

* * * *

Later on in the evening Jimmie Rezaire strolled down into the bar and thence into a lounge sprinkled with palm trees and wicker tables. He did not want to do anything except savor his freedom. He intended to dine well and to go to a theatre. He thought pleasantly upon feminine companionship as a man does who has been in prison for a term...

Then he saw Vivienne.

The shock of seeing her again almost made him stagger. Vivienne! He had often wondered during his prison days where she was. He had known at his trial that she had got away with Sam on the launch—his launch—safe to France. Then nothing more.

Yet there she was, attractive as ever, dark bobbed hair, wide-set brown eyes with that alluringly foreign look in then depths. At her elbow was a cocktail and by her side a fair-haired young man in a well-cut blue suit.

Jimmie Rezaire advanced. As he came across the lounge Vivienne looked up and met his gaze. A man far more modest than Jimmie could not have failed to see the interest that sprang to her eyes. With a word she dismissed her companion who vanished obediently before Rezaire reached the corner.

"Jimmie!" she cried. "What luck! I was wondering how I could get in touch with you. I knew you were just out," she added, in a lower tone.

"Well, Viv, you're as lovely as ever," replied the man as he took the vacant chair. "And I mean it. You've got a..."

"Jimmie, boy, before you say another word, I must thank you from the bottom of my heart for the way you helped me before you got pulled by the police. You saved me from Holloway."

"Forget it!" said Jimmie briefly. "That's all behind us. *I'm* going to forget it."

"I should think so. But the way you diddled 'em all the time was wonderful. I read about your doings in the English papers while I was over in Paris just before you—you went away." She paused delicately; it is bad form among certain classes to talk openly of prison.

"What are you doing now, Viv?" asked Jimmie changing the subject.

"Shop-lifting on the grand scale," replied the girl sweetly. "Me and that young fellow, Harry Hyslop, you saw here. We've got some great schemes on. He's a good lad; plenty of go. Sent down from Oxford for forgery or something and now he's in our game. But what are you going to do? ...Say, it is fine, your being out again. Like old times." Her eyes suddenly grew soft. She had known Jimmie very well indeed in the old days.

Jimmie Rezaire ignored the sentimental turn she had given. "I don't know what I'll do," he said seriously.

"Why don't you start a Private Inquiry Agency?"

Jimmie lay back and laughed for a full minute. Viv always had a little joke. Then he stopped. The idea was not so bad after all. With his knowledge of the underworld and of thieves' methods, and above all with his clever and original brain, he could do well. It ought to give him all the excitement he wanted.

"Might—if it came to the worst," he said at last.

"Or Secret Service work? Lot of money there."

"I did something in that line once," said Rezaire reminiscently. "But"—he turned and faced the girl—"are you trying to make me run straight?"

She lowered her eyes. "Well, I don't want you to be put away again. I'd—I'd like to see something more of you."

"So you shall," he grinned. "I'm going to laze for a bit. We'll have a high old time together."

"Where'll your money come from, Jimmie boy?"

"You know. Paris. All my Robinson-Carlyle game's takings. I...why, what's up?"

"Haven't you heard yet then?" she gasped much concerned. "Why, of course you can't have"

"What?"

"Sam!"

"Sam! Where?" Jimmie instantly displayed fright. At the moment he feared Sam's vengeance more than anything else in the world. "He—he's in the States, isn't he?"

"Oh yes. *He's* away all right. But that money of yours in Paris. He got away with it. Found out about it from some papers of yours in the launch, forged the signature, and drew it all out. He knew you wouldn't hear anything about it till you came out, and couldn't do anything when you did."

Rezaire sat silent for some time. This was a blow. His plans for a wide and joyous holiday had vanished. And Viv was right; he could do nothing. An ex-convict cannot very well invoke the law to regain ill-gotten money from another and vanished criminal whom the police were already seeking for worse crimes than forgery. He laughed shortly. It meant he would have to alter his ideas, for he had not much of a bank balance in London. Money had suddenly become a pressing necessity.

"Well, that ought to square Sam and me," he said at last with forced hopefulness.

"Sam doesn't think so," answered Vivienne soberly.

"But…" Jimmie began once more, feeling the old fear of Sam's vindictive cruelty.

"Oh, don't let's talk about that ugly beast!"

"You had a row with him, eh?"

"Yes. Tried to get off with me in Paris and I said I'd put the police wise to him. So he pushed off to New York. I draw the line at living with Sam."

"You got a friend now?" asked Jimmie delicately.

"Nope," returned Vivienne with a hint of encouragement. "Hyslop's only a business partner."

But Jimmie was again lost in thought. This affair of money was a nuisance. He would have to find something lucrative to do sooner than he had intended. He suddenly recalled the seedy man of the park seat and his offer from some person or persons unknown. Might do worse. He looked at his watch. He decided he would ring up after all and see what it was. He might get a hint or two about something good. Jimmie knew there was always a lot of big money knocking round for those with originality and daring. He turned to Vivienne.

"Where do you live, Vivienne?"

"Flat in Maida Vale," she said, and added: "By myself."

"Well, money or not, I'm going to celebrate my first evening out. We're going to have dinner at the Savoy and do a theatre and then dance."

"And then?…" queried Vivienne softly, looking at him out of her dark foreign eyes.

"Then I'm going to sleep like a log on a real bed for once," returned Jimmie lightly. "I've got a room here. I'm Ferguson by the way, Mr. A. J. Ferguson… Now you run off and change. Meet me at the Savoy. And," he added catching sight of the young man in the blue suit seated at the far end of the lounge, "tell your little partner in crime he's not on in this act..."

"Oh, H.H. is quite tame," replied Vivienne carelessly as she rose. "A promising boy too, as I said. In fact," she added as an afterthought, "you might do worse than think up some game for the three of us."

* * * *

At a quarter to eight Jimmie Rezaire deposited Vivienne at a secluded table in the Savoy Restaurant and with some curiosity rang Park 8465. He was answered by a common little voice.

"'Ullo, who's that?"

"Who's there?" asked Jimmie wondering what he could find out.

"Who's that, I said?" repeated the voice guardedly and Rezaire smiled as he answered.

"I want to speak to a Mr. Jack."

"Oh." A subtle change took place in the tone. "'Arf a mo'..." He heard a rustle of paper. "Here's a message! Will you be at the top of the steps leading up from The Mall to Waterloo Place at ten-thirty tomorrow the 12th?"

"Whom am I to look for?"

"I dunno. Gent said he'd know *you*."

The receiver went down with an air of finality.

Jimmie Rezaire smiled again. A less clever man would have been baffled by the whole incident. Not so Jimmie. He guessed its meaning fairly accurately and his opinion of the unknown went up. Park 8465 was an obvious accommodation number, probably some small tradesman, Jimmie shrewdly surmised, who took messages to hand on to inquirers for Mr. Jack or John or whatever the password might be. Nothing to be learned: nothing to give away. A cleverly conceived arrangement. As he went back to Vivienne, he realized he was in touch with someone big.

CHAPTER II

MR. NEASDEN

Jimmie Rezaire waited on the steps below the Duke of York's column and looked out over the autumn tints of St. James' Park. It was a beautiful morning and the money question was worrying him less. He felt at peace with all the world and was smoking a cigar. He had enjoyed to the full his first evening's liberty and had danced with Vivienne for a large part of the night. He had also told her a little of his proposed venture; but she had argued against it.

"You don't know who they are, Jimmie," had been the gist of her reasoning. "They're quite likely to be some international jewel-gang who want someone to climb out on."

"Don't you believe it. They'd have chosen some mug," said Jimmie. "They wouldn't have waited for me. Honestly, Viv, I'd back my grey matter against most people's." He was not boasting when he said this—he was merely stating what was to him a fact. Certainly so far in his career he had outwitted by sheer originality and mental daring those who had come up against him.

"Well, anyway, I don't like it," had retorted Vivienne, and, "Well, anyway, I've got to have money," Jimmie had countered.

And there he was waiting at ten-thirty…

A man passing down the steps with a cigarette unlighted in his mouth stopped near Jimmie Rezaire fumbling for a match. Jimmie perceived the old game at once and was not surprised when the other, politely begging a light, added:

"Good morning, Mr. Rezaire. You are on time, I see. Permit me to introduce myself—Mr. Neasden."

"As good a name as any," smiled Jimmie closely studying the other. He saw a tall, spare man, loose limbed and with a big but narrow head. The nose was large and arched in the Roman type, the eyes set close together, the lips were thin and clean shaven. A very clever man, thought Jimmie to himself. Aloud he was politely replying that he would be delighted to walk down The Mall and discuss matters of mutual interest.

"Of course," the strange Mr. Neasden said—he spoke in a refined and pleasant voice—"you will excuse our meeting under these circumstances, but you realize I don't want you to know anything about us—should you not fancy our proposal. In my—er—little party we believe in being impersonal."

"Exactly," replied Jimmie.

"I ascertained when you were coming—er—out of retirement and had you followed, because to tell you the truth, Number One was rather keen to get you with us. He was much impressed by your ability during the events that led up to your seclusion. As you know, everything came out in the papers. The way you fooled the police was superbly conceived—if I may say so." He chuckled to himself. "To hide, as a common drunk at the price merely of next morning's fine, in the very camp of your enemies, Vine Street, was a delightful whimsy. Quite after my own heart."

"Thank you," returned Jimmie curtly, wondering when the fellow would cease his pedantically polite flattery and come to the point. All this he could see was pose, a defence to conceal the man's real personality. Quite possibly, he himself was this mysterious Number One he had mentioned.

"Now I gather you are free—open to come into any business?"

"Yes," replied Rezaire briskly. "I am free to come into any business, as long as there's good money in it."

"There is. Heaps. Hard cash. And I may add, you will play to a large extent a lone or rather a directing hand."

"That is what I expect," put in Jimmie, feeling he had better impress himself in his turn.

"You don't mind what you do, I suppose?"

"I draw a line at murder."

"Oh!"—the other appeared a trifle pained at this social shortcoming, as though Rezaire had said he didn't dance. "Well, I take it you have no love for the police?"

Rezaire merely chuckled.

"Dislike capitalists?"

"Like to help 'em part."

"You're not particularly patriotic?"

"I don't think so."

"Good. Then you don't really mind what line you take up?"

"If there's money in it and if I work—more or less—on my own, I'll come in on practically anything," said Jimmie decisively. He had been scrutinizing the other during the conversation and put him down as a really clever crook, a good man to work with and a dangerous enemy. He wondered what his line was and asked.

Mr. Neasden smiled slowly.

"We-ll," he said, "we-ll, I fly very high. What would you say to a high-class burglary campaign, each affair carefully planned out beforehand and for a definite object? There are many gentlemen in foreign countries who are willing to pay well for certain valuable articles, such as pictures, manuscripts and the like, which but for our efforts would not come on the market at all. Collectors have no morals." He shook his head. "But we can't talk here, though you see I trust you. Will you consider the matter and meet me tonight at a more convenient place, with your decision?"

"Certainly," agreed Rezaire. "Where?"

"Well, I find a restaurant is always good," answered Neasden in his pedantic manner. "There's a little place in Soho, in Warsaw Street, called the *Coin de Paradis*." He described the way to it. "Will you be there at 9:30 tonight, after dinner, and I will be along. Go to the room upstairs; and I should advise you to order a quarter flask of the Old Red Chianti; I can recommend it. Good day!"

Jimmie Rezaire watched him as he moved off with a long shambling gait. Then he drew at his cigar once or twice and threw the butt away. Finally he whistled with mingled amusement and surprise. Burglary on a cultivated scale was the game then. A lot of money to be made there with properly worked-out plans. Anyway, he had practically made his decision. But,—a little furrow appeared between his eyes,—he wondered if he were wise. Neasden was a peculiar man, and under his pose of long-winded politeness, a dangerous customer. His quick gaze had noticed a crease in the other's coat running from the bottom button to the side pocket, as though that pocket generally held something rather heavy. Jimmie did not like dealing with people who habitually carried heavy things in their side pockets. Jimmie was a man of peace; he abhorred physical violence because the very thought of pain made him afraid.

He spent the rest of the morning in various financial transactions. At the end of them he discovered that his assets were a bare two hundred pounds. That would not last long, thought Jimmie, for he liked to live well. The sooner he got something lucrative to do the better, and he viewed the stranger's proposal in a more enthusiastic light.

* * * *

Rezaire lunched with Vivienne and her young partner, Harry Hyslop, at a restaurant near Leicester Square. The meal was lively, for they had a table in a discreet corner. Hyslop, who turned out to be quite a humorist in his way, described to Jimmie the latest dodge they had worked in their "shop-lifting" campaign.

It certainly was a clever trick and had resulted in the acquisition of two valuable fur coats. Jimmie was much amused. He also conceived a certain patronizing admiration for Hyslop. At first he had thought him sloppy, both in looks and in his fatuous manner of talking, but under this exterior Jimmie soon found a clever and well-educated young man. Indeed, an ideal subordinate for any daringly-conceived job. The more Jimmie studied him, the more he wondered how on earth he could ever have worked with Long Sam when he might have got hold of a young chap like this.

They all stayed talking in the restaurant for a long time after their meal was over. Before Hyslop and the girl went off on some further business Vivienne sent out for an early edition of the evening paper and found something about their latest exploit, which she read with much amusement.

"Why don't you come in with us, Jimmie?" she asked. "It's a paying game! Or work up a scheme for us all to go in on?"

Jimmie shook his head, smiling at the tribute to his organizing ability.

"He flies higher than us, H.H.," remarked the girl to her partner.

"And works on his own?" queried the youth.

"Sometimes," agreed Rezaire.

"I mean"—Hyslop seemed to have reciprocated from his lower status Jimmie's admiration—"I mean you wouldn't want a chappie to work under you, what?"

"Well, at the moment I'm thinking of going in with someone big."

Vivienne's eyes narrowed. She looked at Jimmie, seemed about to speak, remembered Hyslop, and didn't.

Rezaire guessed the question and said: "I'll tell you more about it tomorrow, Viv, if you'll lunch with me."

"Right ho… Well, so long, old thing." She and Hyslop went off leaving Jimmie smoking thoughtfully at the table, and smiling to himself. A resourceful girl that, clever as well as attractive. And the boy was all there too. He picked up the paper she had left and read of their handiwork again. Then his glance strayed to another item.

"THIRTY THOUSAND POUND PICTURE ROBBERY."

"GEMS OF LORD STAMPING'S COLLECTION STOLEN."

"*At dawn this morning the historic mansion of…*" Jimmie read with interest. He found himself wondering whether this might not be a job of Neasden's gang. It seemed to bear out what the man had said, and he knew there were "syndicates" which undertook the theft of famous pictures on which unscrupulous collectors had a predatory eye. If so, it must be a paying game and he felt glad he had decided to accept. Then he saw lower down a statement that the theft was probably the work of a gang from America, to which country it was presumed the picture would ultimately travel, according to a preconceived plan. He left the picture robbery, attracted by a big headline adjoining:

"ANOTHER R.A.F. FATALITY."

"H'm," thought Jimmie, "always killing themselves. It'd take a good bit to get me up in a plane…"

He was about to fling the paper down when an interpolated heading "MYSTERIOUS LOSS. SPIES IN ENGLAND?" caught his eye lower in the column. The word "mystery" was to Jimmie like a horn to a hound. He skipped the details of the accident,—apparently a plane flying early that morning at Duxford had crashed in a field close by—and read the last paragraph.

> *"Some considerable mystery attaches to the accident, as the two officers were, it is understood, testing a new and highly technical apparatus for bomb-dropping invented by Professor J. Murchison, the details of which have been kept secret by the Air Ministry. When the wreckage of the machine, however, was investigated this important apparatus was found to be missing. There were few spectators of the mishap, it being but shortly after dawn; but Mr. Hodgkins, a farm laborer, who was presumed to have arrived first on the scene reports that while he was still one field away he saw a man dressed in grey also running towards the wreckage. He lost sight of him owing to an intervening hedge, and when he arrived this stranger was not there. Mr. Hodgkins thought little of it at the time, being concerned with extricating the dead men; but it is now believed possible that the unknown detached the apparatus (which may or may not have been damaged) and made off with it. It has been known for some time that certain individuals were desirous of obtaining information about this important secret. An attempt was made two nights ago to enter the hangar, and suspicious characters have been reported near the airdrome. The police are anxious to get in touch with anyone who observed a man in grey, perhaps carrying a parcel or a strange portion of machinery about one foot square, who…"*

At this point Jimmie became aware of a man tapping his sleeve. It was the waiter intimating that at three-fifteen luncheon clients could be dispensed with. Jimmie yawned, threw the paper aside and left.

* * * *

It was nine-thirty when Jimmie Rezaire turned out of brightly lighted Shaftesbury Avenue, doubly bright by reason of wet pavements and a drizzle that caught and magnified the lamp rays. Rounding another corner, he was in Soho—that queer little piece of South Europe squeezed down into the middle of London. His hands were deep in his pockets and he was sauntering along with a cigarette between his lips casting glances of keen enjoyment to either side. He had by no means finished savoring the pleasure of being a free man.

He had ascertained that Warsaw Street, in which was the *Coin de Paradis* restaurant, led off Greek Street next beyond Bateman Street, and he soon reached the corner and turned into it.

It was a darker and narrower street than Greek Street he noticed, containing a few shops, shuttered at this late hour, a coffee bar, and many common little houses with an indefinable Italian air of secrecy about them. Some way up the street to the left he saw a lighted sign bearing the name he sought. Surveying the dark, wet street, almost deserted at this hour, he approved the choice of meeting place.

He looked at his watch. He was a trifle late, but he had sat long over his dinner. Luxurious and civilized meals were still an unutterable delight, as long as he kept his mind off his bank balance.

He was nearly at his destination when without warning from a courtyard opening into the street just ahead of him and about three or four doors before the frontage of the *Coin de Paradis*, a man staggered out. In a muddled way he saw Jimmie and made for him, lurching in inebriated fashion. Rezaire drew back a pace, but the other came on, and was only two yards away when he pitched forward with a maudlin cry, his outstretched hands scrabbling at Rezaire's feet.

"Well, he's pretty far gone," thought Jimmie and suddenly was aware of another man who had run out from the courtyard after the reveler, but had stopped at the sight of a stranger. "Friend of yours?" he continued out loud. "Tight as a lord, he seems."

"Yes, yes, isn't he?" agreed the other effusively and bent over the man, who was still lying as he had fallen face downward. "Must loosen his collar," he added.

Rezaire made as if to help but the other said hurriedly: "No, no, it's all right."

Jimmie stood back and watched him curiously. Some little incongruity in the scene struck him, but before he could put a finger on it he noticed that though at first the newcomer had loosened the other's collar as he had said, his hands were now running busily over the recumbent figure, as if searching him. Good Lord, he thought suddenly, he's going through his pockets. He was about to remonstrate, when the other rose quickly to his feet as an obvious loafer attracted by the unusual sight came up at Jimmie's elbow.

"Tight as a lord," repeated the little man and stood looking down at the figure. His back was still towards the nearest lamp and his head was bent so that his face remained in shadow, but he seemed to be pulling nervously at a moustache with quick jerky movements. The rain fell gently. More people arrived murmuring curiously, but did not interfere, a drunken man being primarily the business of his friends. No one attempted to move him.

"Well, we ought to put him in shelter," suggested Jimmie kind-heartedly. "He'll get his outside soaked as well as his inside. Give a hand," he added to those about him.

Two or three bent to the figure and moved him, with lolling head, to a door-step. Other passers-by added themselves curiously to the group. A woman suddenly said in broken English:

"He ees ill—seeck! *Pas ivré!*"

Certainly the figure's face was deathly white. Jimmie stooped closer. A vague and terrible suspicion slowly took shape…

"Gor!" suddenly exclaimed a man behind him on a note of horror, one of those who had lifted the young fellow. "Gor!" He was staring incredulously at his hand, "*Blood*! 'E's been done in."

The murmur of the crowd rose to a horrified chatter in three languages as it surged convulsively inward.

"Good God!" cried Jimmie, looking at his own hands. On one of them were smears, while on the pavement, distinct even in the shadow cast by the encircling onlookers, was a dark smear slowly merging into the surrounding wetness of the rain.

Before anyone could say more, a policeman, who had been passing down Greek Street, was among them, a shiny caped figure of law.

Jimmie, an inquiry on his lips, looked round for the little man who had been with him first. To his amazement he found he was no longer there. He had disappeared into the wet night. He questioned eagerly, but no one had seen him go. With a shrug of the shoulders he let the matter drop. It was not his affair. He tried to edge away himself, but the voice of the policeman detained him.

As if by common consent the crowd stood back while the constable after a brief examination of the body dispatched a bystander for an ambulance, drew out his note-book and began to question Rezaire.

* * * *

At the end of three-quarters of an hour it was all over and Jimmie, after explanations at the police station, was breathing again. For one ghastly minute he had thought that within a couple of days of emerging from prison he was finding himself accused of murder. But he was quite safe. The testimony of the onlookers, and particularly that of a woman who had been at an opposite window, had made it quite clear that he had never touched the man up till the moment when with the others he had lifted him to the door-step. Suspicion had naturally fallen on the small moustached stranger who had followed the dead man out from the passageway, and had so obviously snatched at the suggestion of drunkenness. The police were already searching for him on the only slight description that was supplied, for neither Jimmie nor anyone else had seen his face in the light.

As he walked rapidly away from the police station, Jimmie cursed his luck. As the principal witness, he was involved in the affair up to the neck, just when he wanted to keep clear of anything to do with the police. Not only had he had to disclose himself as an ex-convict to the Station Sergeant and the Inspector (though he was pleased to see they were impressed by his identity) but he had also thought it best to explain—when asked for his name and address—that he was at the Grand Cross Hotel under the name of Ferguson. This was annoying in that it meant he would have to change later if he wished to conceal himself properly for any other purpose of his own. Most annoying of all, he was now late for his appointment with the mysterious Mr. Neasden. Indeed, by this time the restaurant was probably closed.

He turned again into Warsaw Street and looked for the *Coin de Paradis* sign. It was not visible; it had been switched off. Underneath the restaurant was dark. Jimmie swore with feeling. It was long past ten-thirty and, as he had guessed, the place had closed for the night. Thanks to this infernal business he had missed his meeting.

He walked on to the point where the dying man had fallen. There was a policeman on duty there, with several staring loafers whose curiosity was stronger than their dislike of the rain. There was also an obvious reporter and down the passage whence the dead man had staggered, which he now saw was a *cul-de-sac*, called Jewel Court, with a few doors opening into it, there was a detective making an inquiry at an open doorway.

Jimmie passed the entrance to the courtyard and came to the restaurant about fifteen yards beyond. Though the ground floor was dark there were lights in the first and second floor windows, so Jimmie, after a moment's thought, knocked at the door—though without much hope. There was no answer, but the policeman turned and looked at him.

"Want anything?" he asked coming up to him.

"No," said Jimmie as pleasantly as he could. He had not yet got over his dislike of police. "Just wondering if I was too late. It's not quite eleven yet."

"Ten to," replied the constable curtly.

"Is there a side-door to this restaurant anywhere? In that courtyard back there perhaps?" asked Jimmie. Since the first floor light was on he considered it quite possible Neasden might be waiting there yet and that there was another entrance beside the main one.

"No, there ain't," retorted the other with finality. "They're all private doors down there and anyway my orders is not to let anyone past 'cept belonging to them houses."

Jimmie moved off without a word. He was annoyed about the whole matter, and wondered what was the best thing to do. Then he decided he would phone Vivienne that he could not lunch after all and would revisit the *Coin de Paradis* tomorrow at lunch time and if unsuccessful then at the same hour next evening, trusting to Mr. Neasden's common sense. He was not sure that he wouldn't have to change his mind about accepting Neasden's offer—at any rate till this murder had been finished with; for he knew he was in for a busy time with the police, owing to the ill-luck that had made him so important a witness.

He regained his hotel in a vile temper. As he undressed, his mind reverted to the events of the night to which hitherto he had not given much thought, except in so far as they had upset his own plans. He found himself wondering why the young man had been killed.

The investigation had revealed that he had been viciously stabbed in the side with a thin stiletto the handle of which had snapped off with the force of the blow. It was a mortal wound, and yet the murderer had followed hard on his heels and, seizing on the suggestion of drunkenness, had under pretence of helping a friend searched him thoroughly. Evidently, therefore, he had followed him because he was anxious to obtain something—something presumably incriminating—otherwise he would not have been so rash as to run out into the street behind his victim.

Out in the street! Jimmie suddenly stopped his toilet and said "Ah." He had just recollected what the incongruity was which had subconsciously caught his attention. Neither of the two men had been wearing a hat. For a supposedly drunk man this had not struck him as unnatural, but for the other it had. It pointed to the fact that the pair must have just run out from inside a house. The clue, Jimmie decided as he got into bed, would almost certainly be found behind one of the doors of that *cul-de-sac*, Jewel Court.

But that was the business of the police. Jimmie laughed. He wasn't going to help them, except to clear himself of any suspicion. He had seen quite enough of the police from the other side of the fence.

CHAPTER III

SECRET WORK

At an early hour next morning Jimmie barely awake was told by a page that two gentlemen particularly wished to see him. Could they come up or would Mr. Ferguson come down?

A little later in a small room leading out of the lounge Jimmie Rezaire was facing his two men visitors. One he could not place, a keen-faced young man of about thirty; the other was obviously a plain-clothes man from Scotland Yard. Jimmie, breakfastless, was feeling ill tempered. He could see what that infernal affair last night was landing him in for—interviews at all hours of the day and night, visits to police stations, unending repetitions of his story.

"Well?" he said shortly. "You don't leave me alone much, do you? You had me put away for I don't know how long without asking after my health, and yet the minute I get out you're after me—this time wanting my help."

"That's about it," said the detective pleasantly. "But I hope you're being good. I see you're here as Ferguson."

"It's because I am being good," lied Jimmie swiftly, "that I'm here as Ferguson. Rezaire is a handicap to honesty."

"Well, we won't bother you for long, Mr. Rezaire. I'm Detective Inspector Gullidge of the Yard and this gentleman belongs to the British Secret Service. You may call him Captain Smith. He'd like to ask you a few questions about last night's murder."

"Secret Service, eh?" Jimmie whistled. "Has someone killed a spy?"

"Other way round," put in the stranger. "The dead man, I'm afraid, was a friend of ours. Now, Mr. Rezaire, I'll be brief. It is possible that this man had secured just before his death some information of great value to us. Did he say anything at all to you when"—he glanced at a paper which Jimmie saw was a copy of his last night's statement—"he fell dying at your feet?"

"Not a word."

"Give you anything? A paper?"

"No."

"Was he carrying any parcel or box? Or any odd package?"

"Nothing."

"H'm! Look here, Mr. Rezaire, I don't want to be nasty, but I know you have no cause to like police or Secret Service men. You *are* telling the truth now, aren't you? This is a very big matter. Something highly important has momentarily got into the wrong hands, and you've chanced on an edge of the game."

"I'm straight with you," said Jimmie slowly. "I've got nothing against Secret Service. Hate 'busies' though," he added for the detective's benefit.

"This is a big business," repeated the other, as if hoping Jimmie might yet disclose something.

"I know nothing," continued Rezaire unperturbed. "You will remember from my statement that the presumed murderer went through your man's pockets?"

"I know. He must have got away with anything there might have been. There was nothing of importance when we searched the body; we've unpicked every stitch."

"Well, can I help you further?" Jimmie was quite unconcerned. The business failed to interest him. He stared at the ceiling and relaxed comfortably.

"Afraid not." The other was clearly disappointed at the poor results of his interview. "But if by any chance you remember anything of interest that isn't in your statement, you can get in touch with me through Inspector Gullidge. And—pardon my mentioning sordid details—our rewards are high."

"I know. I did a job for your people once."

"Did you?" asked 'Captain Smith' with some interest.

"Yes, I did," replied Jimmie. With a curt nod he concluded the interview and went in search of food.

Police at any time were distasteful to him, but police before breakfast...

* * * *

With some eggs and bacon and coffee inside him Jimmie felt better. Life to him looked rosier and even a policeman was no longer a blot. Always fond of excitement, it seemed he was having his share. Besides the invitation extended to him by Mr. Neasden, (with whom by the way he had yet to get in touch) there was this Secret Service drama for which he had suddenly found himself in the front row of stalls. A very big matter, 'Captain Smith' had called it and had added mysteriously that something important had got into the wrong hands. Jimmie was not really interested but he speculated for a moment on what that something might be. Probably, if the Secret Service were concerned, it was plans of some sort. New types of submarines or guns or tanks were always being invented and there were always spies and nations who would pay heavily for information of new designs or new armaments,—particularly Russia, who, striving professedly for peace, was secretly making ready for war. Rezaire knew there was always far more activity in espionage circles than the public knew; and during his life before prison he had often come across traces of it, had even taken a hand once. And now he had stumbled into some of it again. He almost wished he had stumbled a little deeper. He would have liked to have taken a hand once more; for there would certainly have been a chance to make big money. Anyhow, he thought, as he went upstairs to dress with more care after his first hurried toilet, he was in on something else as good, as soon as he could get in touch again with Neasden. He rather fancied himself organizing thefts of valuable pictures and works of art for sale to unscrupulous collectors. It was an enjoyable idea.

Upstairs Jimmie Rezaire was just spreading out the wet trousers he had worn the previous night when his eye caught a gleam of white. He looked closely and saw there was something in the cuff of one trouser leg. It was a folded bit of paper. Wonderingly he drew it out; then gave a little start as he recognized a blood-stain. For a moment his brain moved rapidly; then suddenly he recollected how the dying man had seemed to scrabble at his ankles just before his life went out...

Jimmie Rezaire got up at this point and locked the door. A little smile was on his lips, as he recalled 'Captain Smith's' inquiries. Very carefully he unfolded the paper and examined it.

One side of it he dismissed with a glance; it merely bore the word "Cheese" written in a round hand, either in indelible pencil or perhaps struck off on a duplicator in faint purple ink. But this was only incidental, of minor importance. The point was that the back had been used for rapid notes in shorthand. At two places this shorthand fragment was obliterated by a blood smear, obviously caused by the dead man as he folded it up to dispose of it. He must have been doing that even as he staggered out of that *cul-de-sac*.

Jimmie's eyes were gleaming with excitement. He had realized that he held in his hand a clue, and an important one; that in fact, he possessed what 'Captain Smith' had guessed might be in existence and had been searching for. He squared himself to the table with the paper in front of him and set himself to decipher the faint shorthand. Luckily it was Pitman's, which he knew.

He transcribed the first two words and then whistled aloud in overwhelming amazement. He had indeed happened on to a big thing. For the words were "Murchison sighter."

The paragraph in yesterday's paper about the Duxford accident leaped to his mind. The stolen aiming apparatus invented by Professor Murchison. The mysterious man in grey who had been first at the wrecked airplane. The newspaper had hinted then that spies were in the neighborhood attempting to secure information about the secret and that the lucky opportunity of the accident had given them what they wanted. And it had been true and the Secret Service were after it. No wonder 'Captain Smith' had said it was a very big matter. Trembling with excitement he set to work on the remainder of the shorthand.

After a quarter of an hour he leaned back and surveyed half a sheet of note-paper, the result of his labor. It read:

> "*Murchison sighter hidden in London. Corona. Slight damage only, but thieves unable understand principle. Decided own experts must examine.*
>
> "*Intention take it Paris hand to man spoken of as Siminski for transport Russia. Possession earlier than thought—so Siminski not due Paris till 19th.*
>
> "*Gather going openly Calais on 19th. Delay also necessary for passport difficulty*" (here came the blood smear obliterating the next words).
>
> "*Gang unknown. Not Carlo's. Three possibly four.*"

At this point the writing was again smeared and then came to an end. It looked doubtful whether there had been more, though the paper was a part of some card of which the upper and larger half had been torn off. Luckily the shorthand writing had been on the lower half of the back. The whole thing showed signs of having been jotted down in a great hurry as though the writer had suddenly realized that he would not be able to give his information in person, and had no time to give any but bare details. It was without doubt genuine; its appearance and the manner of its disposal proved this.

Jimmie Rezaire stared at the paper for some while. His busy brain was exploring many avenues. His first thought had been to get in touch with the Secret Service immediately and demand good payment for the delivery of this important clue. But now a new idea took shape: could he not do better out of the affair than that? He was in a unique position, for not only had he been present at the man's death and actually spoken to his murderer, but he now held in his hand information which presumably not even the murderer knew he possessed—for the dying man had played his part skillfully to the last with that fall and his scrabbling fingers.

Good Lord, he told himself, only a minute ago he had been expressing regret that he had not been more deeply in this secret service affair, and now he was the very center of it. Why—the idea came as a flash—why could he not take on the business himself? There would be a good financial reward for getting the Murchison sighter back and for catching the spy-gang; and, he brazenly told himself, he had as good a brain as anyone.

No sense of duty bothered him in the matter; he had no feeling that he ought at once to hand over his knowledge to those in the proper quarter better qualified to deal with it. He was out for what he could get. He knew he was in a strong position; he held strong cards and he meant to use them to his own advantage. The only problem was how.

He frowned at the paper a moment longer. It was not as clear as he would have liked. It would mean hard work, perhaps dangerous work, and for a moment he hesitated. Then the thought of the money came to him again and turned the scale. Of course it all depended on 'Captain Smith' but Jimmie knew that if he held out, 'Captain Smith' could have but one answer to his proposal.

He spent a minute or two memorizing the facts contained in the precious paper; then putting it away in his pocket, he unlocked the door and went down to telephone to Inspector Gullidge.

* * * *

Within an hour Rezaire was sitting with 'Captain Smith' in a small private room somewhere in Scotland Yard.

The young man's keen face looked more worried than when Jimmie had seen it earlier that clay; but there was a hint of excitement in his first swift "Well?"

Jimmie went straight to the point.

"You were asking me whether I had any information from the man who was killed."

"Ah," said 'Captain Smith.'

"Then you had after all?"

"Pardon me. I did not have then."

"You mean," said 'Captain Smith' quickly, "that you have now?"

Jimmie thought rapidly. He realized the situation had to be handled carefully, that he must compel the man opposite to accept him as an ally, and yet create no feeling of antagonism. It must be done delicately, and Jimmie said slowly: "No, I do not mean that either. What I have now, and did not have before is merely knowledge which I think may lead to something more definite."

"But this knowledge," said the Captain, "belongs to us."

"It can't," Jimmie replied hesitantly. "Not without a great chance of destroying whatever good it may do."

"You realize that you would be well paid?"

"I am thinking of that."

"Well, at what price do you value this information that you possess?"

"It isn't information that I possess," Jimmie repeated. "It is merely the possibility of information, and the only way that it can be of value to either of us is for you to accept me as an ally, and yet allow me to work it out as I think it should."

He paused there and said deliberately, "You know the man in the grey suit at Duxford and the secret bomb-sighter?"

"Hello," said 'Captain Smith' and appeared to consider. "So you know what we are after. That's interesting."

"Yes; the Murchison sighter."

"Do you know where it is?" he flashed quickly.

"Nope," said Jimmie carelessly. "Wish I did, but the information I hope to secure may help me to find it."

"Look here. This is all very well," said 'Captain Smith' with a harsh note in his voice, "but we can't work completely in the dark. The thing may be leaving the country even now..."

"En route to Russia," finished Jimmie sweetly. "See what a lot I know? But don't worry. It's not going out for six days. I gather success wasn't expected so soon, and their plans are not rounded off."

This continued display of knowledge upset the Secret Service man.

"Oh, stop play-acting," he said. "You don't realize I can force you to divulge whatever you know. Right now, if I want."

He moved his hand to a bell.

"Force me," said Jimmie, lightly. "You can't *force* something of which I'm not sure myself. All force can do will be to kill whatever chance I have to help you. I told you I want this job. I'll play fair with you, and I am not acting."

"Look here, the police can catch you as an accessory."

"Perhaps; but you won't allow it, because you'll frighten your birds away."

"You can't come butting in..."

"I am in already."

"You don't even know all the circumstances."

"I know the important ones. I should expect you to tell me anything else necessary."

"Why should I? You might be one of this gang for all I know—trying to keep us quiet."

"Then I shouldn't be asking you for information. Anyway, I'm in the main drama. You've only seen the curtain-raiser."

'Captain Smith' suddenly laughed at the other's coolness. Rezaire, he perceived, was a clever man. For the first time he began to see something in this offer.

"Look here," continued Jimmie, bringing all his powers of persuasion to bear on the younger man. "Be reasonable. You must realize I'm the only man who can take on this job for you. In the first place, I've done secret service work before—in the Rene Mescaut case of 1919 which you can verify in the proper quarters—and I was commended too. Secondly, I'm the only fellow except the murderer who was, so to speak, in at the death—in itself a big advantage. Thirdly, I've a chance at an important clue. Fourthly, if you'll look up my criminal record, you'll find that, whatever people thought of me, I was never considered stupid. What do you say to all that?" The other was silent thinking it over. He was young and beginning to feel impressed by Jimmie's personality. Also there was much truth in his remarks.

"I'm offering myself as an agent for you with all these assets," resumed Jimmie as he perceived the hesitation. "I start with many advantages. In return, I require any further information and help that you can give."

"There's a good bit in what you say," admitted 'Captain Smith' at last. "But I haven't authority to…"

"Well, Captain Smith, speaking as man to man, will you go and obtain it? You'll only lose if I don't take the job on. It's no good appealing to my patriotism and it's no good trying to bluff me. I'm making you two square offers," he continued. "First to restore this missing Murchison Sighter—"

"Before it's too late?"

"As long as it's in England it isn't too late. You must know as well as I do," he added remembering the dead man's notes, "that such a complicated thing can only be understood by experts. And photography is no good in this case. So it'll have to go to their own experts in Russia."

"That's true."

"And my second offer is, if possible, to round up the spies concerned. For each item, I expect a financial reward—without strings—payable as usual on results."

'Captain Smith' thought very hard for a moment digging the point of a pencil into the tablecloth. At last he said:

"Well, will you wait here for half an hour or so?"

"Right!" agreed Jimmie. "Good man! I'll wait. Back to the Secret Service again, eh, as Kipling might have said."

Jimmie waiting in the empty room was confident he had achieved his objective. Those to whom 'Captain Smith' was now referring could not help but see the strength of his position. He was so obviously the only person—as long as he refused to give up the information, he had the whip hand. As for his having been a criminal—well, on this sort of job it was an asset. And this job would be far better from the point of view of quick returns than joining up with a syndicate of picture thieves. Which reminded him he must get in touch with Mr. Neasden and his Number One, and tell him he had changed his mind after all. He did not wish suddenly to ignore his offer without a word of explanation. All criminals were suspicious and all criminals—especially a syndicate—were dangerous, if they thought they had been deceived. Neasden in particular looked a nasty customer.

When 'Captain Smith' returned, their conversation was resumed, but this time in a highly different atmosphere. 'Captain Smith' had verified Jimmie's previous work and had been authorized—albeit reluctantly—to give him any information and help he required and a free hand. It was realized he possessed all the strong cards. The Secret Service was not often held up like that; but Jimmie Rezaire had done it.

Jimmie settled down to listen…

There was not much of importance that 'Captain Smith' could tell him, beyond that the dead man, (who had been on the watch at Duxford) had by midday yesterday succeeded in getting onto the trail of the man in the grey suit. This man had without doubt skillfully removed from the crashed plane the ingenious little Murchison sighting apparatus which was in process of being taken up by the Air Ministry.

"An infernal bit of luck their getting hold of it like that," said 'Captain Smith' whose tone was now quite friendly. He even felt a little respect for Rezaire after what he had learned from his chief. "We knew of course someone was after it, but we didn't reckon on it being dropped at their feet yesterday morning. And the whole thing will go in a parcel ten inches by twelve."

"I read about it in the paper yesterday."

"Yes, that blasted *Evening Wire* got hold of the story. I think it'll be hushed up now though. And the police, by the way, have been told to treat last night's murder quietly; so you won't be bothered much with that, and your name has been suppressed!"

He resumed the story of the theft, telling Jimmie how at five P.M. yesterday they had received through a reliable channel a curt message from the dead man, stating that he was in London and asking for six men to meet him at nine-thirty at an agreed point, but that he had never turned up. The next they heard, he had been killed.

"Here are the details of what was found on him and so on. Nothing important."

'Captain Smith' gave Jimmie a paper. "As you know, he was stabbed to death with a thin stiletto of no particular design—there are hundreds like them in Soho—but there was also a slight flesh wound caused by a revolver bullet. The peculiar thing about that is that it must have been fired from below. We've rounded up a couple of doubtful characters who are in the spy game, but it's not them."

Jimmie could not resist saying in an offhand manner, "No, it's not Carlo," just to watch the other ineffectively concealing his surprise. His remark brought the expected reaction.

After remarking with a new respect that Rezaire certainly seemed to know a bit, 'Captain Smith' gave him another paper, this one the full results of the police inquiries at the four doors which opened into that *cul-de-sac*, Jewel Court, whence the murderer had come.

"Numbers 1 to 3 are, you will see, as innocent as the air—too many different people, strangers, living in each house. One man—his name's down there—swears he looked out of his window and that the court was empty a bare two minutes before you saw the two men emerge, which makes the business more mysterious."

"What about Number 4 then?"

"They're the only ones who are at all doubtful, but only on the slender ground that they're all Italians from Verona. But they have a good record all of them."

Rezaire continued to listen in silence, gathering all the information he could, for he saw he was going to have a busy time. He was disappointed, however, in the Jewel Court houses. It seemed obvious that the murderer, emerging from the passageway, had just run out from inside a house; and Jimmie had been relying on one of those houses to supply a clue. But perhaps Number 4 might yet do so.

He asked a few final questions and then got up. "I hope you won't ask me to this place again," he said. "It smells too strong of policemen for me."

'Captain Smith' laughed. "It'll be too risky for you, once you get going after this crowd. They'll probably get you anyway."

Jimmie thought that rather in bad taste and asked stiffly: "How can I get in touch with you?"

"Only through Inspector Gullidge, I'm afraid," smiled 'Captain Smith.' "But he'll get me quite quickly and he has instructions to help you at a moment's notice. Well, good luck! By the way, of course we're trusting you and we're not going to shadow you or anything like that, but we hold that this—er—forced arrangement with you will not prevent our carrying on any line of investigation of our own. And then, of course, it is possible the Special Branch will stick their fingers in."

"I understand."

As Jimmie walked out into Whitehall, he reflected with a grim humor that whereas three days ago he had been in prison, he was now almost a detective, with the confidence, albeit compelled, of a Secret Service man and with an Inspector to give him help if he wanted it. He had done well to hold out for this job himself. It would be difficult, but well worth it both in interest and in reward.

CHAPTER IV

THE COIN DE PARADIS

By one-fifteen Jimmie Rezaire was at a table in the upstairs part of the *Coin de Paradis*. The restaurant was like others of its type: a heated lower room with paneled walls, crowded tables, a desk with a stout lady behind it, and an all-pervading smell of frying oil; while in the upper room, (reached by a short passage from the narrow staircase which thereafter continued up into the private portion of the building) the formula was repeated, without the smell or the stout lady and with fewer tables set further apart. A wonderful place that upper room for conspirators to foregather, thought Jimmie. One could talk without being overheard by neighbors, one could stay on without exciting comment, and one could come again and again without appearing in the eyes of the proprietor anything more than a customer who liked the cooking.

He had scanned the lower room for Neasden and then, in spite of evident dissuasion, had insisted on mounting to the upper. It was empty of customers, but after a moment a small and obviously Italian waiter appeared from below for his order.

"Give me the lunch," commanded Jimmie, waving away the proffered card. "And a quarter flask of Old Red Chianti," he added, remembering the suave Mr. Neasden's advice.

"Sairtanly, sair." The waiter bustled off.

For a moment Jimmie stared after him. He felt he had seen his face somewhere before. But where he could not say. Then he dismissed the matter from his mind and began to wonder whether Mr. Neasden, realizing that he must have been prevented from coming last night, would have the sense to come again. He did not like to make inquiries from the waiter or proprietor; because obviously the less the restaurant people knew about doubtful customers who met there the better. He was also wondering how best to explain to Neasden that he did not wish to join him after all. For of course the high-art burglary business was now off; or at any rate till he had finished with the problem of the stolen Murchison sighter. That would occupy him fully for the next week.

He settled down to his food, but his brain was busy marshalling his information about the sighter. What had he definitely learned from the dead man's shorthand notes? A certain amount at any rate. He knew that there were three if not four men concerned. He knew that the bomb sighter was hidden somewhere in London. He knew that because it was so complicated the secret was safe, and would remain so till it left the country for Paris, where the man Siminski would arrive on the 19th to take it to Russia. He knew that therefore he presumably had six days—for today was the 13th—six days during which the spies apparently had to make some arrangements for ensuring a departure without a hitch by the Calais route. Of course they might try to smuggle it out by means of a motor boat or airplane, but the boldest way was always best; a passport, a suitcase and an innocent appearance would do the trick easily.

He recalled the mysterious word "Corona" which had also been in the dead man's notes, but could make nothing of it. Some clue was contained in it, but what for the moment he did not know. At the moment it might mean anything or, perhaps, nothing.

He took a draught of wine—it certainly was good—and sat back with a furrowed brow. His deductions all seemed to him logical; and it was reasonable for him to suppose that this information which he possessed about his opponents' plans, was at the moment correct. The question was, would they alter them? After consideration Jimmie decided that, unless they grew suddenly scared, they would not change—since at the moment they had every reason to suppose their secret had not leaked out. That deduction, too, seemed logical.

One other thing was certain, that the spies would be found somewhere in the Soho neighborhood; for everything pointed to the fact that the dead man had acquired his information close by. Actually, Jimmie felt fairly sure that a clue would be found in a Jewel Court house, for men do not go about on rainy nights without hats unless they have just come from inside a house; and two minutes before the Court had been empty. He began to formulate a plan for getting in touch with the inhabitants of Number 4 house—the ones who were "doubtful."

His close-knit chain of thought was interrupted by the entrance of a man—the long expected Mr. Neasden. He came over to Jimmie's table with a smile of welcome, and his nose looked even larger in the tiny room than it had outside.

"Well?" he said and some of his suavity had gone leaving hardness underneath. "Where were you last night?"

"Couldn't get," replied Jimmie briefly, annoyed by the other's tone. He paused deliberately to let his annoyance become apparent and then added: "I was unfortunately detained by the unexpected."

The close-set eyes on either side of the large nose studied him for a minute. Then Neasden replied with a laugh: "It doesn't matter. We shouldn't have had time to talk." He remained standing. "As a matter of fact, I haven't any time now. I…something has made me rather busy today."

The waiter appeared, placed the bill of fare on the table and hopefully pulled out a chair, but Neasden waved him impatiently out of the room.

"Before I go," he continued. "Have you thought about our proposal?"

"I have."

"Well, do you wish to come in with us?" Jimmie decided the moment was ripe to explain politely that he could not join. He opened his mouth to do so and then something happened which made him shut it again. After a brief moment of furious thought he nodded pleasantly and said, "Of course I do," as though the idea of refusal had never been in his mind.

For in that brief moment his eye had fallen on the menu which the waiter had just placed between them. Something about it seemed familiar, yet he knew he had never entered the place. Then he had realized. At the bottom of the list of courses, under the sweet, the word "Cheese" was written in a round hand and in faint purple duplicating ink. In fact, the fragment of paper on which the all-important shorthand notes had been scribbled was a portion of a menu card exactly the same as the one before him. His brain worked rapidly. In a flash he realized that the dead man must have visited this very restaurant on the night of his death, that there was probably a clue to be picked up by discreet inquiries in this secretive-looking upper room. Yet if he said "No" to Neasden, it would be difficult, if not dangerous, for him to continue to visit the place, after having refused to join the syndicate.

So he had nodded pleasantly and had said: "Of course I do."

It was not till after he had committed himself that he realized that in his eagerness to probe the mystery of the Murchison sighter, he had involved himself definitely with this Number One and his burglary syndicate. In fact, he had apparently let himself in for playing a game of deception. But the chance had been too good to miss. In no other way could he have been so free to visit without comment both the *Coin de Paradis* and Jewel Court, between the pair of which he was convinced some clue to the mystery would come to light. The risk was certainly worth taking.

Neasden, who had evidently guessed nothing of Jimmie's rapid thoughts, was continuing surprisingly: "I'm afraid I lied to you yesterday when I told you high-class burglary was our game."

Jimmie stared in amazement. Pie had not expected this.

"That was Number One's order in case we couldn't trust you," explained Neasden. "Number One leaves little to chance and we don't like traitors, though we have drastic methods with them if necessary. Without boasting, I may say, the 'methods' are very satisfactory."

Jimmie found himself murmuring assent, though his heart had begun to beat rapidly at the word traitor. For a moment he felt inclined to back out before it was too late. Then he recollected that after all he was not really intending to play the traitor. By the 19th his own job would be settled one way or the other and he could consider Neasden's proposals—even though for the next week he had to avoid taking a definite part.

"However," Neasden was saying, "we will discuss our plans tomorrow night. I dine here most nights—though tonight I have other arrangements."

"Am I to meet this Number One?" asked Jimmie curiously.

"I'm afraid not. He prefers to remain unknown for the time." He turned, paused as if he had remembered something and came back.

"We shall all be very glad of your help." He spoke as if Jimmie were contributing to a charity. "Your skill and knowledge will be of inestimable value to our party."

When he had gone, Jimmie sat back and considered this strange, loose-limbed man with the pedantic method of speech. He was certainly cultivating a pose, cultivating, too, an obvious flattery. Jimmie did not like him. He was clever underneath; and yet he was not the leader. Again he found himself wondering who Number One might be, the organizer of this mysterious syndicate.

* * * *

Jimmie experienced his first set-back that very afternoon. Re-reading after lunch the information with which 'Captain Smith' had supplied him, he had been forced to the conclusion that the police inquiries left Number 4 Jewel Court as the only possible house from which anyone might conceivably have run out on that night. From this he had decided that the occupants must know something about either the dead man or his murderer. So he had knocked at the door and explained that he was acting for a cinematograph company who wished to take a news-film on Monday of the site of the murder and of the occupants of the adjoining houses. He had felt certain that the answer to this proposal would give him a clue; for people who were connected even remotely with a murder would be most anxious not to be photographed, under any pretext, even though they had come safely through the police questioning.

The response, however, had baffled him. The entire household, all at home on Saturday afternoon, had greeted his news with acclamation, had chattered incessantly in Italian and had displayed such intense eagerness to be photographed as often as Jimmie liked, and even with the corpse if it could be obtained, that he could doubt neither their innocence nor ignorance. Yet he remained positive that when the two men ran into the street from Jewel Court, they had come not so long before from inside a house. He was nonplussed.

He crossed Warsaw Street and looked straight back into the Court. Houses composed it on all three sides with their four doors opening onto the paved courtyard. Reliable evidence now showed that no one had come out of those doors, for the results of the police inquiries at Numbers 1 to 3 had been incontrovertible; reliable evidence also stated that the courtyard was empty two minutes before the dying man staggered out. From whence, then, had he come? It was a puzzler, Jimmie admitted, for he could not have popped up through the paving-stones or dropped from the sky...

At this simile he suddenly whistled to himself and recrossed Warsaw Street. There was a drain-pipe running down the side of one of the houses from the roof. Ten feet up Jimmie detected a fresh scratch on the paint. A man might have stabbed another up on the top, pursued his dying victim down the drain-pipe and finally out into Warsaw Street. In this way all the evidence would have been satisfied. And if they had come hatless from the roof, they had probably come from a window opening onto the roof. This new theory thus threw suspicion on any house of those between the drain-pipe side of the courtyard and the end of Warsaw Street. Altogether about a dozen including two macaroni shops, the *Coin de Paradis* restaurant and a public house at the corner of Warsaw and Frith Streets.

The *Coin de Paradis*! He whistled again. That restaurant seemed to play a big part in his thoughts. He thought of the paper he had found and suddenly saw, as clearly as if he had been told, the nature of the Secret Service man's death, perceived why it was on the back of a *Coin de Paradis* menu that he had written his hasty notes. Other gangs, besides Neasden's, had found that deserted upper room a good meeting place and it was there that the unfortunate agent had tracked the spies. He saw him dining—no, more likely concealed near by—scribbling down the main points of what he overheard, discovered, dashing out, the way perhaps barred to safety below, and so upward, out onto the roof with his precious information, caught as he reached the drain-pipe, getting down into Jewel Court though mortally wounded. The shot would have been fired perhaps as he raced upstairs, thus explaining why it came from below; but once outside, the silent stiletto was the weapon used. Poor devil! Then the murderer, having put Jimmie off the scent, mingled in the crowd and vanished back into the near-by restaurant. Yes, Jimmie saw it all as clearly as if he had been told. And a further deduction was that, quite possibly, the proprietor of the *Coin de Paradis* was not entirely ignorant of strange things that went on in the upper part of his premises.

He stared meditatively at the drain-pipe which had led up to all this chain of thought for a little longer, then suddenly turned and sauntered off. He did not wish to attract attention. He would have liked to climb that drain-pipe to see what attics or trap doors opened onto the roof—particularly those from the *Coin de Paradis*. But that was impossible in the daytime, and probably at night too. Because a man had come down, it did not follow that one could go up. The easiest method, mused Jimmie, of gaining access to the roof would be through a window opening on to it… At this point he had a sudden idea, begotten by passing the public house at the corner of Frith Street, called "The Vine," which presented to the world a grimy card inscribed "Beds for single gentlemen."

In a few minutes he found himself talking to the proprietor of this hostelry, a surly and uncommunicative Englishman. To him he represented himself as a Frenchman—Jimmie could speak French perfectly and broken English with conviction—looking for a bedroom. Did M. le Patron have one unoccupied in his beautiful hotel?

"M. le Patron" was used to foreigners. He explained the prices on his fingers and then led the way upstairs. Jimmie declined the first room offered, for it opened onto Frith Street; but on the top floor he found what he wanted. It was a room at the back with a dormer window opening onto a short length of sloping roof. Ahead of him for forty or fifty yards below stretched the dingy back premises of the Warsaw Street houses, till Jewel Court jutting backward intercepted the unlovely view. And an agile man could scramble from the window of this top room to the grey-slated line on the left, at the foot of which what appeared to be a narrow drain with a low parapet ran along the whole length of the Warsaw Street roofs—one of them the mysterious *Coin de Paradis*.

Within a short space Rezaire had paid a deposit and departed "pour mes valises."

* * * *

The more Rezaire considered the coming night's adventure, the more nervous he became. Eventually he visited a shop he knew near the Strand, whose owner did not bother overmuch about police and regulations. Here he purchased an automatic and ammunition, but not even the possession of a weapon made him think less apprehensively of his intended exploration that night along the roofs of Warsaw Street. One man had already met his death up there; suppose he himself encountered one of the spies? It was quite possible,—no, it was even probable—that the murderer would return under cover of darkness to search the roof and remove incriminating evidence, in case the police came to any awkward conclusion about the drain-pipe. Tonight would be the spies' first safe opportunity of doing so. They would not have attempted it in the daytime for fear of watching eyes, and last night a policeman had been on duty in Jewel Court. Besides, on that occasion they had probably dispersed as soon as possible. The more Jimmie considered it, the more likely it seemed to him that when darkness fell, the murderer or his companions would be upon that roof to clear up any traces of the crime. Dared he be there too? He thought again of a thin-bladed stiletto stealing in between his ribs.

On return to the hotel the sight of Vivienne and Hyslop gave him fresh courage—a courage that he knew was only temporary—for he realized his own limitations. Bold enough in conception of plans and daring in carrying them out, yet fear of physical pain or death crumpled him up. He had felt the same about Sam and his knife; thank God Sam was away in the States! He looked admiringly at Hyslop as they chatted perfunctorily while the waiter brought them tea in the lounge. Hyslop had half his brain—if that; and yet Hyslop was not afraid of knives.

An idea came to him. Why not get Hyslop to join him that night? Or better, join him in the whole business. Only yesterday he had been considering Hyslop as an ideal subordinate for a daringly conceived job, while Viv, a good judge, had spoken well of him. He was up against a gang and would need help from someone before the end. And he certainly wasn't going to get it from the police if he could avoid it.

"Well, Jimmie," said Vivienne, when the waiter had vanished, "why did you call off my lunch?"

"I had to see that fellow and give him my answer."

"Good. I'm glad you're out of that."

"I'm not out of it. At least, nominally I'm not. Viv, I've been having the hell of a time since I saw you..." He told them briefly about the murder and the Secret Service man's visit.

"What rotten luck getting mixed up in that!" was Viv's comment, otherwise she did not seem greatly interested.

Rezaire paused to drink some tea and consider finally whether he should tell them anything more or not. Then, his mind made up, he bent quickly forward and said:

"Look here, you two! I tell you I'm on to something big."

"What? With this bird you lunched with?"

"No, my only reason for saying I'd go in with him was to leave me free for this big job."

"Be careful!" began Vivienne. "If you start double-crossing…"

"I've taken on some Secret Service business," continued Jimmie paying no attention.

"What?" cried Vivienne.

"Go on, old boy! You don't mean it!" ejaculated Hyslop.

"I do. And it won't be dead easy, either. Look here, I shall want your help, Hyslop, if you'll come in with me; yours too perhaps, Viv. In fact, here's that job for the three of us you were asking for a day ago…

The tea was cold in their cups before Jimmie Rezaire had finished his story. To Jimmie's delight, Hyslop was wildly enthusiastic. He, it turned out, was fed-up with shop-lifting stunts; the one thing, apparently, that he wanted in this world was to go roof-climbing, as he put it, with Jimmie that night. He recognized that there was a probability of meeting the murderer and even hoped they would—and though Jimmie didn't see eye to eye with him, the young man's enthusiasm drove away his previous nervousness.

Vivienne, on the other hand, was definitely scared. Not, she admitted, of the spies, but of the deception Jimmie had committed himself to with Neasden.

"I'd rather go down for five years than be caught double-crossing a gang," she reiterated. "It's not worth it—not even for the advantage of continuing to visit that restaurant. And this Number One business frightens me too," she added. "It generally means there's someone big in it, when his associates don't know his name. I don't like it, Jimmie!"

In the end Jimmie grew exasperated, largely because he felt instinctively that she was right.

"Oh, hang it," he said. "I'm not necessarily going to play tricks. I shall be free of this show in a week and then I can carry on with Neasden."

"But Jimmie…"

"And anyway the damage is done now. Besides I want the cash."

He signed to Hyslop, and prepared to leave. He had to get a suitcase to take round to his new bedroom at "The Vine." Also it would soon be dusk and Hyslop had suggested that it would be a good thing to get out on the slates before anyone else. He explained that if, as Jimmie thought, there was a likelihood of a clue, he didn't see why they shouldn't get it themselves, as well as reconnoiter the roof.

"After all, old lad," he drawled, "getting hold of this jolly old bit of machinery isn't the whole show—financially that is. I mean to say, we want to round up this performin' troupe as well, don't we, what?"

Jimmie agreed and they went, leaving Viv reluctant but committed to give what help might be required of her.

CHAPTER V

THE CLUE ON THE ROOF

Night had just fallen when Hyslop scrambled silently out onto the short slope of roof beneath Rezaire's attic window. Inside the darkened room was Rezaire himself, his heart beating uncomfortably fast, though his nervousness had been slightly allayed by the presence of his cheerful companion.

Soon a low signal from Hyslop told him it was his turn. He crawled out backward and, feet in the gutter and hands on the slates, edged carefully along to his right. In a few minutes he had joined his companion at the corner, from which point the roof of the Warsaw Street house ran in a shadowy line towards the back-jutting mass of Jewel Court.

"We're lucky," murmured Hyslop, indicating a narrow but flat drain which offered a good pathway between the roof-slope and a low parapet. "No more gutter-perching, what!" He showed a white grin in the darkness.

Jimmie grunted in answer and on rubber-soled feet led the way along this path, crouching to support himself with his right hand on the parapet. He carefully scrutinized each attic window as he passed. About half-way along he came to one with closed wooden shutters, and this Hyslop, by cautiously climbing up the roof and down the far side towards Warsaw Street, quickly verified as belonging to the *Coin de Paradis*.

They made a careful examination of it in silence and soon Jimmie nearly gave a little cry of triumph. Under the tiny circles of light from their carefully sheltered torches there was plainly visible on the wooden window-ledge a small stain of blood.

"The revolver shot," whispered Jimmie exultingly. "This settles it." The connection between the dead man and the *Coin de Paradis* restaurant, assumed by him from the menu card, was at last proved.

After a moment they went on, following what Jimmie surmised had been the route taken by those other two on the previous night. Twenty yards on, the line of roof turned at right angles, but catlike Jimmie went straight on up the slope, Hyslop at his heels. Letting himself down on the far slope, he came upon a similar flat drain and a parapet, over which he at once cautiously peeped. He found himself looking down into Jewel Court. A short distance to his left, and only a foot or so below, was the top of the drain-pipe he had noticed that afternoon. His theory then must have been correct. By that means had the murderer and the man he pursued come so mysteriously into the *cul-de-sac*.

He whispered for a moment to Hyslop, who was obviously impressed by his clever deductions; then his eyes caught a scrap of paper in the drain. He picked it up, holding it close to his eyes in the dim light reflected from the street below, for he did not like to use his torch on this side of the roof.

Then came a little exclamation of triumph. The fragment was grimy and sodden with rain, but he could just make out the pictured heading of the *Coin de Paradis* menu. And it was not complete; in fact, it was the larger half of the piece that had been thrust into his trouser-leg the night before.

"Then that proves no one of the jolly old performin' troupe can have been up here since that poor devil was done in," said Hyslop, when Jimmie had explained what it was.

"That's how I figured it. They wouldn't have left this about, if they had. I'm glad we got here first."

"Hope they don't meet us here…" continued Hyslop. "Not that I would mind a scrap, but I mean to say they'd get suspish' and run this Murchison gadget out of the country before we get a smell of it."

Jimmie did not answer for a moment. Thinking of the same thing—the fact that their chances of success would be ruined if the spies realized they were themselves being spied upon—he had had a flash of genius.

"Look here!" he whispered quickly. "Look round and pick up any information you can, but for God's sake don't be seen. I'm going back to my room for ten minutes. I've had the hell of an idea… Tell you later… but I must do it before anyone comes up."

He slipped like a shadow up the roof behind and was gone, leaving Hyslop peering down into the paved pool of light that was Jewel Court, from where there now rose voluble Italian voices—probably the excited inhabitants of Number 4 discussing their forthcoming appearance on the films.

* * * *

Back in his room Jimmie pulled down the blind, switched on his torch in the shelter of the bed so as to screen it from the window, and crouching on the floor examined his find minutely. The front, as he expected, showed all the courses except "cheese," and bore, moreover, under the heading at the top, the date, Friday the 12th, the night of the murder. Without doubt it was the missing portion. On the back nothing was written, or if there had been, it was now washed out by the rain. But Jimmie had not really expected any further information. He had a far better idea and he chuckled at his own cleverness as he pulled a pencil from his pocket and carefully blunted its point on the iron of the bedstead. Then after a moment's consideration he set to work to write hurriedly on the back of the menu in shorthand, imitating as far as possible, the style of the jottings on the other half and taking care to lend his handiwork an appearance of a day and night in the open air.

Jimmie had long ago realized that his sole chance of success depended on the gang of spies keeping to their plans and so securing for him the advantage of the information he held; and his present object was to insure their doing so. True, they presumably were not aware that he held this knowledge; for the murderer had seen with his own eyes that his victim had died before he could pass on anything. Yet by searching the body he showed that he suspected the other of obtaining information of *some* kind. The question for the spies, therefore, at the moment was: How much had the Secret Service men found out, and where was this knowledge? Jimmie proposed to answer these questions for them by letting them safely discover, if they cared to search the roof that night, the information the dead man had obtained, and—further to allay their fears—wrong information at that.

In a few more minutes he was creeping back along the roof with the fragment of menu-card in his hand. Scribbled very faintly upon the back—indeed, that there might be no doubt of its genuineness it would almost take an expert to decipher it—were the following notes:

> "Tracked thief of Murchison to London as reported.
> "Just discovered this is a blind. Murchison sighter not here but believe hidden in East Coast town. Yarmouth?
> "Intention go out of England by secret motor launch to Germany before end of next week."

And, thought Jimmie, that ought to make the mysterious gang realize the unlikelihood of the dead man's having passed on any information, and that, even if he had, it would have been false.

He listened carefully at the *Coin de Paradis* window as he passed, but heard nothing. Moving on to the corner, he deposited his paper carefully at the foot of the roof. As he was doing so he encountered Hyslop, coming softly down the slates and carrying something carefully wrapped in a handkerchief.

"What's that?"

"Show you later, old boy," whispered Hyslop.

"At the moment I don't think we ought to hang around too long."

"Yes, you're right."

They turned back, Jimmie leading. As he again reached the shuttered attic window, he suddenly stopped dead, turned round to Hyslop, his finger on his lips, and began to steal past with infinite caution. For between the shutters there moved a thin ray of light—a torch. That a person should use a torch in a shuttered room suggested to Jimmie that whoever it was was presumably intending to open the shutters and venture out. In other words, this was exactly what he had anticipated, an expedition by the murderer or another of the spies to remove anything incriminating from the scene of last night's chase.

Hyslop bent down and put his eye to the chink to see if he could learn anything about the identity of his opponents, but Jimmie signalled to him urgently. It was too risky.

As they climbed silently under the blind into Jimmie's dark room, Hyslop held up his finger. Listening intently, they heard a faint creak—as of a wooden shutter being pushed slowly open.

"Only just in time, dear old fellow," muttered Hyslop.

"Don't light the light," snapped Jimmie, hearing the rattle of matches.

"Not a fag, old boy?"

"Not unless you chew it!"

Hyslop laughed shortly; then:

"What was your game with that bit of paper?" Sitting on the bed in the darkness Jimmie told him briefly and Hyslop was delighted at the cleverness of the idea. "Dashed good wheeze! And now they'll carry on just as they've already planned?"

"That, it seems, is our one chance of success."

"I wonder who the devil this little lot are and what they're like! ... I say," Hyslop sprang up. "I've got an idea. Let's get out on the roof again, get over to the far side—the street side and see if we can catch a glimpse of this chappie who's out there now?"

"I don't think it's much good," demurred Rezaire, rather scared at the thought. "It's too important a business to risk getting spotted, and if a couple of us are scrambling..."

"I'll go alone then," volunteered Hyslop. "I can move as silently as a dumb shadow!" Jimmie began to see merit in the suggestion. Hyslop might learn something of value and on the far side of the roof would run little risk of detection by their enemy. In another minute Hyslop had vanished into the outer darkness.

* * * *

Hyslop crept silently back after a lapse of half an hour, devoted by Jimmie to a hard reasoning out of the whole affair. The young man was very dirty and very excited.

"Had a grand time," he said. "I lay on the far side of the roof hanging on to the ridge and popped the old head over at intervals. I saw the fellow at the attic, a fairly sizeable chappie too, and the first thing he did was to clean off those blood stains,—I heard the sandpaper. Then he moved along, found your little bit of ground-bait and put it in his pocket. He looked fearfully bucked about it."

"Was he armed?" asked Jimmie uneasily.

"I think he had a gun—with a silencer on it as far as I could see. It was too jolly dark to make out much. Then he climbed up the other roof like we did and down to the part looking over Jewel Court; but he was too late there…" Hyslop broke off to chuckle.

"Too late?"

"Oh, of course I haven't told you yet. I mean *I* had already got what was to be found there, old son."

Jimmie remembered the object wrapped in a handkerchief which Hyslop had been carrying and which now lay on the table. He examined the blind carefully and then switched on the light.

"Well, what was it?"

Hyslop paused proudly before replying.

"The handle of a dagger. How's that for clever, old lad?"

"Whew!" Jimmie whistled. "Good man! Where was it exactly?"

"In the mouth of the drain-pipe; on the wire cage which catches rubbish."

"He must have dropped it as he stabbed."

"Exactly. Caught the poor devil at the top, as you said."

Jimmie had an idea.

"What about finger-prints?"

"I thought of that, old boy. That's why I wrapped it in a handkerchief."

"You'll pass all right," said Jimmie, very pleased with the young man. He was all that Viv had said and certainly had brains. If there were finger-prints on his find, they would be invaluable in tracing the murderer. He would get 'Captain Smith,' or that fellow Gullidge, to give it a microscopic examination at Scotland Yard.

"By the way,"—a thought struck him—"I hope there are none of yours on it, H.H., because I want the police to give it the once over?" Hyslop shook his head with a grin. "No fear. I picked it up with my handkerchief by the broken end. Don't want the busy fellows to get a look at my paw-marks."

"Good," praised Jimmie as he undid the silk square and looked at the find. It was an ebony and metal handle, and if it had been dropped by the murderer as he struck might quite well bear a print. Otherwise it was not hopeful. The workmanship was foreign, and with the long thin blade extracted from the murdered man's ribs, made up a slender, cruel weapon, of a type dear to Italians. There were probably hundreds similar in Soho alone.

"I tell you another thing," Hyslop was saying. He produced a small steel tool from his pocket, a cross between a large pair of toothed scissors and an egg-decapitator. "This is a gadget for opening bolts from the outside, provided there's a chink to get it through. It'd take time, but we could probably get through that attic window if we wanted."

Jimmie shook his head. "Good Lord, no! Our whole success depends on keeping them unsuspicious, till we've got a proper plan worked out. If we break in prematurely it'll only scare them."

"Why?"

"Well, after thinking things over my theory is that this restaurant is not only the meeting place but the actual lair of the fellows we're after and that probably they've actually got the Murchison sighter tucked away somewhere inside. Upstairs, I should think, because the lower half seems a genuine restaurant."

"Great Scott. I shouldn't be surprised. They seem to buzz round the place a lot. And I believe the proprietor has bedrooms to let; so people could live on the premises."

"Whether he's in it himself or not, I don't know. Anyway we must get a line on the whole place tomorrow. I shall go and lunch there quite openly. If they suspect me, they'll soon find out that I'm only a criminal and in with this other gang, Neasden's, that meets there. In the meantime, I want you to watch the door tomorrow morning and see if you can tip off who is living there regularly. Can I trust you not to be spotted? Viv told me you were good at disguises."

"Try me!" said Hyslop proudly. "I was a leading light of the O.U.D.S. once."

Jimmie shook his head in mock reproof. "Funny how you 'Varsity boys go wrong! *I* never went to a Varsity, yet here I am a respectable agent of the British Secret Service, while you're living a life of crime."

Hyslop grinned. "As long as it's exciting I don't mind what I do."

"Same here," said Jimmie, then added, thinking of the dagger: "But not *too* exciting!"

CHAPTER VI

A DISCOVERY

Jimmie spent part of the following morning, Sunday, getting in touch with Inspector Gullidge over the matter of the stiletto handle. Gullidge, though obviously jealous of the find, at any rate professionally appreciated the importance of possible finger-prints. Jimmie handed it over to him to be treated and photographed microscopically.

"And," Gullidge concluded, "if there are prints on it and they nick in with anyone in our records, I'm going to pull him in and ask him where he was last Friday night."

"I should see what 'Captain Smith' says first," suggested Jimmie. "It concerns him."

"I shall do what I think best," retorted Gullidge—though he realized Rezaire was right. He turned away haughtily, concluding the interview.

* * * *

Lunch time found Jimmie at the *Coin de Paradis*, passing upstairs with great assurance. On the way he met the same waiter who had attended him the day before, a scrubby little South Italian. Once again he was puzzled by a vague feeling of recognition; but by the time he reached the top of the stairs, he had dismissed it from his mind.

On this occasion the upper room was not empty. At a corner table sat a small clean-shaven man, noticeable for a gap in his front teeth, and with him a fair-haired girl in a startling frock and obvious make-up. The girl was talking in an undertone which ceased momentarily as Jimmie entered, though after a bare second's pause, she continued in a slightly louder voice: "And actually it was her first proposal!"

Clever, thought Jimmie to himself. Had he not been equally smart, the significance of that short pause would have escaped him, and he would have assumed the whole conversation to have been about a girl's proposal. Instead of which it was evidently much more secret. He wondered who the pair were. That they were not ordinary members of the public was certain. They might be two of the very spies he was after; but on the other hand, they might be merely a couple of Neasden's friends and therefore probable co-workers with him in future.

On the chance of learning the real subject of their conversation, he sat down with his back to them. Experience had taught him that people tended to treat a possible eavesdropper less cautiously if he were not facing them. But these two were too skillful; he caught not a word of the murmured talk which ensued except what was obviously intended for him; though after a short while a suspicion grew upon him that the man was speaking in a disguised voice. Every now and then it did not ring true and once Jimmie could have sworn he had heard a certain tone before. While searching his memory for the occasion he unexpectedly came upon something else. The little waiter whose face he had thought he recognized. Wasn't his name Guido and wasn't there some funny business...?

He sent his mind back into his adventurous early days in the under-world. There was a man called Luigi who went to prison—and there was a man who did not go. Everything fell together with a click, and a feeling of triumph came over him. If his recollection served him, then he knew something about the little Italian. In fact, he had a hold on him, the stron-gest hold the underworld knows—the fear of a "shopped" or betrayed companion's wrath. With that as a lever he might make use of this fellow. He would be valuable indeed, a spy in the enemy's meeting place,—if it were not actually their camp, as Jimmie was beginning to believe.

In order to put this scheme into operation, he dawdled over his meal till at last the pair behind him got up and left. Then he ordered coffee and when the waiter served him, he remarked very softly:

"Good afternoon, Guido!"

The other went suddenly white under his swarthiness and nearly tipped the coffee over his client. "My name is Mario," he said in a quick undertone. "Mario Spinello, sir, please. I know no one called Guido."

Jimmie smiled in satisfaction. The other's obvious fear had told him what the words had not. His memory had not been at fault.

"You are Guido Vacchi," he said deliberately; then added in reassur-ing tones: "I mean you no harm. But I know someone who does."

"I have harmed no one, no one at all," protested the Italian, stammer-ing with unconcealed nervousness.

"Ever heard of Luigi?" countered Jimmie and watched him jump like a deer. "Luigi is still anxious to find a certain friend who double-crossed him." Then he continued briskly: "Enough. If you are wise, you'll listen to what I want to say. Where can I have a talk with you?"

"I know nothing of what you speak, sir," cried the man. "Nothing!"

"Well, go and think it over. It's no trap. But," he added sternly, "I warn you!"

The scared waiter left him without a further word and Jimmie stirred his cup reflectively. He believed he had him.

After ten minutes he called for his bill. As he paid, the little Italian, in whom fear had evidently been working, whispered to him that if the gentleman was at Leicester Square Tube Station at four-thirty he himself would be off duty then.

"Good," remarked Jimmie. "You are wise." He gave an enormous tip by way of impressing on the other that he could reward as well as threaten. Then he left the restaurant.

He found, as he walked away along Warsaw Street, that one small thing was puzzling him. The handwriting on the *Coin de Paradis* menu-card had today been changed from the rounded hand in which it had originally been made out. The new calligraphy was angular and upright, in fact, as different as possible. Jimmie wondered if there were conceivably any connection to be traced between this fact and the discovery by one of the spies on the roof last night of the half menu with the false information he had improvised thereon.

* * * *

Guido, an apprehensive little figure in a black felt hat, was already waiting outside Leicester Square Station when Jimmie arrived at four-thirty. Without saying a word Rezaire led the way to a small coffee-shop near by, which happened to be open. Over a cup of vile black liquid he at last began:

"Now, Guido! Listen to me! If you do what I want, I'll pay you. Very well, too. If you don't, well, it won't take me long to get hold of Luigi and tell him where he can find the friend who had him put away for two years."

The little man again went pale at the name and stirred his coffee rapidly.

"What you want with me then?" he mustered, not lifting his glance.

Jimmie paused and thoughtfully lit a cigarette. He had come to the difficult part of his interview; for he did not exactly know what he did want. He was assuming that because Guido was evidently the only waiter allowed in the upper room of the restaurant he knew something about the various people that met there, and might give him valuable information. On the other hand he did not wish to risk betrayal to the spies; for Guido had little sense of loyalty. Though only a pawn in the game, he would need tactful handling.

"You're playing a dangerous game, Guido," he began at last.

"Mario, sir, please!"

"Mario, then. Do you know it?"

"Yes I do, indeed I do. Many times do I say I wish I were out of it." Jimmie had apparently made a good opening. "Oh, to be back in Napoli, with a little…"

"Well, why don't you go?"

"I have so little money, and I owe, too. And I must do as I am told" He hesitated. "*They* also know about Luigi."

"Ah!" Jimmie saw light. The mysterious "They" had the same hold over Guido, or rather Mario, as he now had. And treated him badly too, judging by the recital of wrongs now pouring from the impassioned little Italian—trivial wrongs, mostly, and so of little value, except as an indication that sympathy would be a strong weapon.

He awaited his moment and slipped in a pertinent question.

"What do you have to do for these people?"

"Not to notice nothing," was the prompt answer.

"How?"

"Funny things happen up there!"

"Like last Friday evening?" shrewdly guessed Jimmie, playing his old game of bluff.

"How do you know that, sir?" Mario was completely taken aback.

"I know a lot. That's why you'll be wise to keep in with me," returned Jimmie staring at him. "Go on!"

"If I tell you something," resumed Mario, in a hoarse whisper, evidently impressed, "you won't tell?"

"No, go on!"

"On Friday I was given a little white powder. There was a strange gentleman dining upstairs. I was told to put it in his coffee. Something to make him sleep well, it was."

"Poison?"

"No, a drug. But he guessed and would not drink."

"Gosh," muttered Jimmie to himself. He had indeed struck something, the methods by which the gang of spies put away for a time people they suspected. Then:

"Who tells you to do this, Mario?"

The little Italian hesitated. "The big man," he whispered at last.

"Number One?"

Mario displayed fear. "No, no. I do not know him. He is only a name, but he is terrible."

"Who then? The proprietor?"

"No, he is a fat old fool. I mean the big man." Mario obviously feared to mention names.

"Who? I want to know him."

Mario looked suddenly half-incredulous, half-afraid; but kept silence. Jimmie gauged his man's state of mind and did not press the question, much as he desired to do so. Whether Mario knew the principals in the spy gang or not, he would not tell. And again there was mystery about this Number One—the man without identity.

He interrogated him further about those who regularly visited the upper room, but got little results. Then a new thought struck him. It occurred that perhaps in his meetings with Neasden at the *Coin de Paradis* he might himself come under the spies' suspicion, and might unwittingly receive a little white powder.

"Look here, Mario," he said sternly. "You will see me at your place sometimes."

"Si, si," nodded Mario, eager to please.

"You must not recognize me." Mario shook his head. "I may be accompanied by the tall man with the big nose…"

The other seemed about to speak, but did not, as Jimmie held up a warning finger.

"If at any time you are ordered to put anything in my coffee, you are to let me know."

"But how? They would kill me, I think, if I told you."

"Fool!" said Jimmie pleasantly. "You will on bringing any drugged coffee to me ask me if I will take '*two* lumps of sugar?'"

"But what…"

"And then I shall know. You understand?"

"Yes, yes. I see now. That is ver' clever. *Two* lumps, yes." The love of intrigue, inbred in the Italian, was suddenly evident. He nodded excitedly, and even appeared eager for a chance to help Rezaire. Small wonder, thought Jimmie, his friend Luigi had been betrayed. "I shall do this for you, sir, and you will forget Luigi, eh?"

"If you're good, yes. If you're not, Luigi will be told where the man is who shopped him three years ago," said Jimmie pleasantly. "On the other hand, I shall reward you well for your help. Here!" He passed him a note under the table and Mario's eyes shone with gratitude. Jimmie knew just how to mingle hardness and consideration.

As they left, Mario said with a sudden flash of insight: "You are a detective, yes?"

Jimmie made no verbal answer. He merely spat. Mario, however, understood and apologized.

* * * *

Brilliant inspiration comes at all times—even in Trafalgar Square. With a loud exclamation, which made passers-by stare at him, Jimmie Rezaire stopped dead in his tracks just outside the National Gallery. A moment later he realized his inspiration was not brilliant at all, at least judged by the high standard he set himself. In fact, as he backed out of the crowd, he was cursing himself for an unutterable fool that he had not thought of it before.

Why on earth, he asked himself angrily, had he persisted in assuming—just because Neasden had originally pretended his game was stealing pictures—that *two* gangs met in that *Coin de Paradis* upper room? How immeasurably dense he had been! He ought to have guessed the truth the moment that he learned Neasden's statement was a lie; or even when he first became suspicious of the *Coin de Paradis*. Why, at their original meeting, Neasden had given him a clue, when he said that "there are many gentlemen in foreign countries who are willing to pay well for certain valuable articles." For "articles" substitute "information" and there it was as plain as the writing on the wall. An international information syndicate—a gang of spies.

He passed his hand across his forehead and found it wet. Other aspects had now occurred to him. He was playing a far more risky game than he had at first thought. He was supposed to be a member of this very spy gang and yet he was secretly out to bring them to book. It simplified matters; but he kept remembering Neasden's talk of Number One and the reference to his drastic methods with traitors. A gust of terror swept across him. He would have short shift if he were discovered. And he had to meet Neasden that night. He wondered if he dared back out.

He mastered his fear and began to walk slowly towards Soho. This new development was of enormous importance. He must talk it over with Hyslop, who had been watching the *Coin de Paradis* entrance in disguise all day.

As he went, he remembered Mario's half-afraid yet half-incredulous look. No wonder Mario had looked incredulous when Jimmie had asked so innocently the name of the "big man"—seeing that it was Neasden all the time.

Jimmie Rezaire turned out of Frith Street and walked rapidly down Warsaw Street on the side opposite the restaurant, without looking at it. A tall thin youth with a dirty face and a slack mouth hopefully offered matches for sale.

"Go away!" said Jimmie, but without sufficient conviction, for the youth followed him expectantly, still holding out three match-boxes.

"Why don't you go and do proper work?" rebuked Jimmy as he reached the end of the street.

"Can't get none, gov'nor," whined the young man. "Ain't 'ad a bite for days." He pursued Jimmie round the corner out of Warsaw Street, and out of sight of the *Coin de Paradis*.

"Your finger-nails are much too clean!" said Rezaire surprisingly. "Otherwise it's good! Meet me at a bench in Soho Square in a minute or two. I've got something important to tell you."

Hyslop grinned momentarily. Then his mouth went slack again and he cringed away as if he had received a final rebuff.

* * * *

A quarter of an hour later Hyslop drifted up to a seat in Soho Square where Rezaire was already reading a paper by the last of the daylight. With a grunt he sat down beside him and also brought out a dirty folded square of newspaper. He did it very well, and Jimmie felt pleased with him. This young fellow was quite an acquisition.

Behind the cover of the two newspapers Jimmie, after apologizing for not having guessed it before, rapidly told his companion of his amazing discovery that Number One's gang was no other than the gang of spies they were after. He had not bothered previously to describe Neasden's appearance, but now that he had turned out to be one of their opponents, he did so minutely.

Hyslop displayed excitement.

"But look here," he said, "that sounds like the chappie I saw dodging about the roof last night, who picked up the bit of paper. It was pretty dark, but I got his head against the light once and he certainly had an enormous beak on him. And what's more, I've seen him today."

"Where?"

"He came out of the restaurant this morning at nine o'clock."

"Came *out* at nine?"

"Yes. And I'd been watching since eight, so it jolly well looks as though he's living in the place."

"That settles it," said Jimmie in low tones. "I'll bet a hundred pounds now that this is their hiding place. They've taken bedrooms above and meet in that upper room. Did you spot anyone else? I'm wondering about Number One."

"A fat little man came out at ten and back at twelve. An obvious Frenchman, but I'm fairly certain he must have been the proprietor. Did you see him at lunch?"

"No. Haven't struck him yet. He must spend his time in the lower restaurant—probably he finds it wise not to notice too much. They'll have got him squared too."

"And then I…" Hyslop was beginning, when Jimmie suddenly interrupted with a curt "Finis! Meet me hotel!"

"What the…" began the less experienced Hyslop and was silenced by a muttered "Shut up" from Rezaire who, with an innocent expression belying the words he had jerked out without moving his lips, had glanced up at the sky and was casually folding up his paper as if he had found it too dark to read longer.

Hyslop had the sense not to do the same, but cast a rapid glance over the top of his own newspaper for the cause of the abrupt transition.

In a minute he noticed a short distance off a little man with a white ferrety face, doing nothing too obviously. In short, they were being watched. Hyslop marvelled at Jimmie, whose eyes apparently let nothing escape them.

In a few seconds Rezaire got up and strolled off. Hyslop stayed where he was, immersed in his paper, in order to see which of them the watcher was trailing.

In a moment the ferrety-faced one drifted aimlessly off in the same direction as Rezaire; so after giving him a full five minutes, Hyslop got up and went to his rooms in a street near the Strand to change his clothes and meet his companion at the Grand Cross Hotel.

* * * *

Jimmie Rezaire without looking round knew that he was being followed, and his brain was busy. He wondered who had set this fellow on to him. It might be Neasden, or it might be some other member of the gang who, not knowing he had been enlisted, had seen him lunching upstairs by himself and had grown suspicious. He fervently hoped he had not been observed meeting Mario, but felt fairly certain he was safe in that respect, for he had taken precautions. Anyway, this follower should be easy to shake off; he couldn't be much good at his job, or he would not have been spotted so easily. Jimmie settled down to it.

He first walked up to Oxford Street. Waited for a bus that was nearly full inside and then took one of the few seats left. The ferrety man, after a moment's indecision, went on top. A minute later at Oxford Circus Jimmie suddenly dismounted just as the bus was starting off again and plunged down the brightly lighted entrance to the tube station. Here he bought a penny ticket at an automatic machine, raced down the moving stairway, dodged under the barrier and got on to the "Up" escalator. He was exactly half-way up again when he passed his shadower, whom these maneuvers had left a little behind, being carried helplessly downward on the other stairway. Jimmie made no sign of recognition, though he would liked to have bowed ironically and taken his hat off.

Outside the station again he turned south and walked rapidly to his room at "The Vine" to change his clothes before going on to the Grand Cross Hotel.

He laughed as he remembered the ferrety man. Why, he thought, did people always underestimate his intelligence?

But in this particular case Jimmie the clever had been outwitted by one who knew his cleverness of old and had allowed for it. The little white-faced man was only a blind to distract attention from the real shadower, a tall figure with a coarsely handsome face and full arrogant lips, who wore a hat pulled down over his eyes. The latter had thus bluffed Jimmie completely, and after watching him into "The Vine" side-door, himself disappeared into the Private Saloon where over a drink or so with the proprietor he at last extracted a small item of information which seemed to please him very much, for he chuckled triumphantly as he finally emerged and vanished in the evening dusk.

* * * *

Half an hour later Hyslop, properly dressed and with his usual vacuous look of gilded youth, was being conducted upstairs to Mr. Ferguson's room in the Grand Cross Hotel. He found Jimmie sitting thoughtfully on the bed staring out at the dark sky through the uncurtained window.

"Who was he?" asked Hyslop, hanging his hat on the bed-post.

"That's what's worrying me," replied Jimmie. "Somehow I feel it's not one of Number One's little lot, because they can't have the slightest grounds for suspecting me yet. You see, they know I am an ex-convict, etc., so it'd be the hell of a mental jump for them to guess I'm now secret service. Especially since I consented quite genuinely to join their gang."

"Quite," said Hyslop encouragingly.

Jimmie got up and pulled the curtain. "Funny," he said reflectively, "if it hadn't been for the Goddess of Chance I might be just becoming one of their leading spirits."

"You are for all you know. You're with the quarry and with the hounds at the same time, old son."

"Always a dangerous game," commented Rezaire soberly. "I'm not looking forward to the dinner with Neasden tonight. He may try and land me in something very definite and I want to... By the way, to continue your report, have you marked anyone else as probably living in the place?"

Hyslop shook his head. "Only our friend with the big beak. I don't think I missed a trick, either."

"H'm. One crook doesn't make a gang," said Rezaire, recalling the "three possibly four" of the dead man's notes. "I wonder who the hell that Number One is. He might be the murderer—in which case he was a little man with a moustache—I wish to the dickens I'd seen his face. And by the way"—he recollected the pair behind him at lunch—"I believe there's a girl, a flashy fair-haired thing, and a man..."

"I saw that girl go in at lunch time—a lively-looking blonde piece—with a little gap-toothed chappie. But I mistook them for innocent customers. They came out shortly before you did."

"That's the pair all right. They were lunching upstairs. They probably live up above too... That reminds me." Jimmie paused reflectively. "Before you came, H.H., I was thinking over a plan for getting a squint at some of those upstairs rooms."

"Get in through that attic?"

"No, you ass. I've told you already that once we let them get suspicious they'd be off like a flash somewhere where we shan't find them before it's too late. That's the reason, too, I don't want to get the police in—which we might do at this point—apart from the fact I don't trust 'em and if they make the slightest slip we're done... No, the Murchison is in that place somewhere, I'm positive, and so is the gang and we've got to reconnoiter the ground very carefully before we strike. Well, this plan of mine... By the way, where's Viv?"

"Coming round here, old boy, at six for a cocktail"

"That girl seems to live on my cocktails," grumbled Jimmie. "Well, we'll go down and wait for her. I've got a stunt for you two to carry out tonight at the *Coin de Paradis*. I shall be there with Neasden but you won't know me, of course."

"Poor Viv'll be scared stiff, old son, when she learns you're trying to nab the very gang you're joining," remarked the young man thoughtfully.

"Why should she? Makes it easier."

Hyslop looked embarrassed. "Oh—er—I don't know, old chap," he said with some vagueness.

CHAPTER VII

A SUCCESSFUL RECONNAISSANCE

Jimmie felt greatly relieved to realize that Neasden was not already waiting in the upper room. It gave him time to collect his composure, for he had been getting more and more nervous of the meeting. Neasden as the spy he was intending to catch was a very different and far more dangerous person than Neasden as a vaguely possible confederate in the near future.

He settled down at a table. Mario approached him without a sign of recognition. At the same window table he saw the fair-haired girl of lunch time, even more startlingly dressed. That she was again there indicated to Jimmie that he had been perfectly right in putting her down as one of the gang. But if she was going to be there all the evening, Hyslop would have to be careful in carrying out his plan—even though he was a skillful actor—for the girl was certainly no fool. Presumably her former companion was not to be with her that evening, as she had already started her meal. To Mario's inquiry Jimmie said he would wait as he was expecting a friend.

He had been there two minutes when a stout little man with a beard, a paunch and" a pair of large-lensed pince-nez came up from below.

"*Pardon*, M'sieu," he began, approaching Jimmie, "but you expect a Mr. Neasden?" Jimmie nodded. "Well, he have telephoned that he is desolate, but he cannot come. Business have called him today to Yarmouth. But—*que voulez vous*?" he ejaculated and spread his hands.

Jimmie instantly looked as disappointed as possible for the benefit of the girl who, he could see, was listening intently. "I'd better go," he said, though nothing was further from his mind.

"Oh, *non*! M'sieu will stay, I hope. I have *e poulet en casserole* Coin de Paradis, tonight."

Ah, so this was the proprietor, thought Jimmie. A Monsieur L. Villon according to a small line of type under the menu head. Hyslop had seen him that morning, but this was Jimmie's first encounter. He covertly studied him under pretext of deliberation. He could not see the eyes behind the thick glasses, but from bushy eyebrows via prosperous middle to patent leather shoes, his whole appearance denoted harmless friendliness. Despite this, Jimmie realized that by no means could he be completely unaware of the dubious character of the two or three customers who met regularly at his restaurant and presumably lived in the rooms above.

Jimmie wondered how much he knew and determined to find out before the end of the evening. It was just possible he could be made use of, as Mario had been; for he looked the kind of man whom a whisper of police and secret service would frighten into submissive assistance.

Aloud he said kindly: "Well, Monsieur, you tempt me. The *poulet* let it be. I hope to come here often. I like this upstairs room."

Monsieur Villon was delighted. "We have some regulars," he said, "and they all come to this room. It is for the regulars. *Que voulez vous?*" he ejaculated again. It seemed to be a characteristic expression of this funny little man. "Mr. Neasden he is a regular. And he ask on the telephone that you will dine here with him tomorrow night instead. He was desolated."

The old man then bowed to Jimmie, wished the girl by the window a courteous "Good evening," and vanished downstairs.

While waiting for his dinner Jimmie wondered what had taken Neasden to Yarmouth. Was it a lie, a blind for other activities? He thought not, for surely Neasden had no reason to suspect him. Or was it something to do with the Murchison? It might be more than a coincidence that Neasden should have gone to Yarmouth the very day after finding Jimmie's faked notes about "a secret launch on the East Coast." Even so, he could not understand his motive.

Rezaire felt he need not have worried about Hyslop's ability to deceive the fair-haired girl. There was no doubt that he was an accomplished actor. His arrival up the stairs in the guise of a young man who had had several cocktails was perfect. With him was Viv, in a very short frock which showed her silk covered knees. She wore also rouge and lip-stick to rival that of the girl at the window table.

Neither of the newcomers gave Rezaire a conscious glance, yet while the proprietor, who looked as though he had tried to dissuade them from penetrating upstairs, was hovering round, Jimmie heard Viv say, "Look at that wet-blanket sitting by himself!" followed by Hyslop's inane bray of laughter. Viv was an absolute artist, thought Jimmie at this. To ignore people completely did not always imply they were strangers—particularly before a clever and experienced observer like the blonde girl,—but to make a remark like that was just right. Moreover, it had also told Jimmie that Viv wanted to know why Neasden, whom she had been told would be there, was not present.

Rezaire finished his course and began to tap idly with his fingers on the table. It was an old trick he had used with Viv before. He saw her imperceptibly enlighten Hyslop; who took his cue and plunged at once into some story about how a fellow had insulted him at the Club. Viv listened ostensibly to him but actually to Jimmie's finger tapping. Satisfied he had her attention, he sent swiftly, "N. not coming tonight" in Morse. Then he stopped. Though there was only the fair-haired spy in the room he did not want to risk anything. She had already been listening with both ears to what Hyslop and Viv were saying. And since, too, she was a member of Number One's gang and presumably was aware of his joining, he was particularly anxious she should not guess there was any connection between himself and the other couple.

Hyslop began to drink champagne and soon began to get drunk on it. Perhaps a little quicker than people usually do, but no one could know how much, or how little, drink he had had before his arrival. Viv also, towards the end of the meal, was giggling loudly at nothing in particular. Glancing up covertly, Jimmie saw to his relief that the fair-haired spy was now merely displaying scornful amusement. Monsieur Villon, however, on his occasional visits to the upper room was looking worried.

Hyslop ordered a second double brandy after coffee and Jimmie observed him pour it away behind a radiator. Viv's arm lay on the table and Hyslop was fondling it in maudlin fashion. Jimmie had never seen such perfect acting. At moments he could hardly believe that all this had been concocted that evening in the lounge of the Grand Cross Hotel.

* * * *

At about nine o'clock, choosing a moment when the proprietor was in the room, Hyslop, who had consumed further drink, rose to go. Suddenly he sat down again with a crash and toppled forward on the table.

Viv was at his side. "What's the matter, dearie?"

"Don't feel well!"

"Of course you don't after that brandy. You come 'ome with me and you'll be all right."

"Yes, yes," put in Monsieur Villon anxiously, while Mario hovered with an overcoat. "You be well at home, eh?" The spy, who had remained at her table smoking endless cigarettes, was still amusedly watching the scene.

"Going to be sick!" announced Hyslop with the deliberation of the drunken man.

"*Non, non*! Impossible," cried Monsieur Villon. "See, I go order you a taxi, yes."

He turned, but Viv stopped him.

"Half a mo'!" she said. "Look! He really is bad." Hyslop's eyes were closed and somehow his face did look like that of a sick man. "*I* don't want to have him really bad on my hands. Have enough trouble with people as it is. Haven't you got somewhere he can lie down for a bit? He'll be all right soon."

The little man almost danced with rage at the bare suggestion.

"He must go. Bah! He cannot stay here. Que voulez vous?"

Viv instantly became vulgar and aggressive: "And why not, please? He's ill! Look at him!" Hyslop groaned and retched realistically. "He'll be all right if he lies down on a bed, won't you, dearie? But you, you old..."

"Let him go to hospital! Let him go home! Let..."

"What, and leave me! No fear!" She raised her voice. "You let him lie down for an hour or so and then I'll take him. Or else I'll make a row."

Monsieur Villon suddenly looked doubtful. A drunken man was fairly easy to deal with. A sick man and a drunken woman were a different matter.

"I b'leeve he's bin poisoned by your brandy," announced Vivienne with hostility. "'S *your* fault. *You* ought to..."

"I shall have the police in," blustered the little proprietor.

"Oh, no you won't. If any police come, *I'll* have them in." Jimmie, watching the blonde girl, at this point saw her eyelids flicker. "He's been poisoned, I believe. You ought to let him lie down. Think I can't pay or what? And you," she rounded angrily on Jimmie, "sitting there smoking and not doing anything to help a lady!"

Jimmie looked confused and murmured something inaudible.

"Yes, I will have the police in," flamed Viv suddenly. "I..."

The girl with the fair hair intervened.

"The man looks really ill, Monsieur Villon," she suggested.

Monsieur Villon apparently came to a decision. He asked to be assured by Viv that if the gentleman were allowed to rest for an hour in a bedroom she would take him quietly away.

"You bet I will," replied Viv vulgarly. "I've got him and I won't let go of him, but I'm not going to be pushed out in the street with a sick toff."

Still talking, though obviously mollified, she helped the incapable Hyslop, groaning at intervals, out of the room, the proprietor supporting him on the other side. With a triumphant feeling which he could barely keep from breaking surface in a smile, Jimmie heard them go upstairs.

"Disgusting, wasn't it?" said a cool voice at his elbow. The blonde girl was looking down at him with a provocative smile.

"These things happen," returned Jimmie looking back at her. Her eyes were very keen and her rude make-up did not really seem to belong to her.

"I saw you here at lunch," announced the girl sitting down opposite with an encouraging sideways glance. "Do you come here often?"

"Yes. I like the place," returned Jimmie guardedly, and they fell into conversation.

Under the pretence of a fair but frail lady trying to make an impression on a solitary man, Jimmie soon perceived that she was questioning him. He grew wary. She was testing him to see if he was trustworthy, assuming probably that he did not know she was a future accomplice. He answered evasively for some time till at last she said with smiling deliberation: "You're very mysterious. Why do you visit this place?" Jimmie could not resist this opening. He leaned earnestly over the table and whispered: "I'll tell you a secret. I'm here to keep an eye on the place. I'm a police officer!"

For a moment she started suddenly; then broke into laughter, as she realized he was making fun of her.

"Oh, in that case," she replied lightly, "I'll say good night!"

As she went out of the door, Jimmie smiled. She had not got much change out of him. What was more important, he hoped Number One would realize from the incident that he was to be trusted. His success would largely depend on his credentials.

He summoned Mario, paid his bill with a tip of ten shillings and by way of refreshing his memory, remarked meaningfully that the coffee had been good.

Mario smiled like a fellow conspirator and murmured: "I will not forget."

Jimmie was just being bowed out when Monsieur Villon reentered.

"Well, good evening. I have dined well," said Jimmie.

"I ask pardon that Monsieur was disturbed by that vulgar woman. But *que voulez vous*?"

"Where is the man now?"

"In the room above. Luckily I have two—three bedrooms here. He is groaning, *sale cochon*. I have left a waiter to watch them both. I do not trust these women, no."

"Quite right. And any trouble gets a restaurant a bad name, doesn't it?" He examined his gloves thoughtfully. "Wasn't there a murder or something not so very far away the other day?"

"Along the street it was," replied Monsieur Villon promptly. "We hear nothing of it till next day. It is a distance. It does not affect us."

"Luckily it wasn't a row in your place," said Jimmie innocently. He brushed a trace of cigar ash from his coat, because he knew it would be of no use looking at those protecting thick spectacles. He had remembered that he still wanted to find out how much the proprietor knew of what went on in his *Coin de Paradis*.

"Oh, the man was not our class of customer," answered Monsieur Villon carelessly. "He was a tramp-man. A low common man. Quarreled, I suppose, with an Italian of hot temper. *Que voulez vous*? But as Monsieur says, it is lucky for our good name it was not here… *Good* evening, Monsieur!"

Liar, thought Jimmie, as he walked away down Warsaw Street. The man had lied obviously in falsely laying such stress on the dead man's not being of his type of customer. It followed then that he most certainly knew about the spies' activities. That he could not be an accomplice was obvious; for spies do not run restaurants, and the *Coin de Paradis* had been going for three years. Jimmie thought of Mario and placed M. Villon in the same class—a timid man somehow in the power of Number One and thus bound to secrecy by fear and money. That was why the spies had chosen his restaurant for their lair.

* * * *

It was not till well after eleven that night that Rezaire, waiting patiently in the Grand Cross Hotel, was called to the telephone and heard Viv's voice excited and a little breathless.

"That you, Jimmie? Are you alone?"

"Yes."

"Well, it worked all right, didn't it?"

"You were wonderful," said Jimmie sincerely, though suddenly there crept unbidden to his mind the memory of the dangers they had shared.

"We found out a lot. I'll tell you tomorrow. It'll do then, won't it? I've sent H.H. home as it's so late."

"What made you late? I've been waiting hours."

"Well, what with one thing and another someone got a bit suspicious."

"Who? Why?" snapped Jimmie. "The show's ruined if…"

"Don't get peevish, Jimmie! It's quite all right."

"What happened then?" repeated Jimmie more calmly.

"After I had done my bit, H.H. pretended he felt better and we sailed off in a taxi. I gave Leicester Square as a destination for anyone to overhear, meaning to change later. But we found we were being followed, so we had to carry on and get out at Leicester Square. The trailer was still there watching and so, sooner than give the show away, H.H. and I went into one of those low hotels in Gerrard Street and took a room there…"

"What?" cried Jimmie.

"It was his idea. *I* didn't know the place," said Viv virtuously.

"Good Lord!"

"Luckily," continued the girl imperturbably, "someone had left some cards behind, so we played Bezique for fiver points for an hour and H.H. owes me seventeen thousand four hundred and sixty pounds. When we came out of course we'd shaken our man off, but thought it safer not to come to you. I'm phoning from Piccadilly now."

"Clever girl!" ejaculated Jimmie approvingly.

"I could tell you everything tonight, if you'd care to come round to my flat in Shrewsbury Court," said Viv after a pause.

"No, tomorrow will do," said Jimmie hastily. "Come here at eleven o'clock. I'm going to sleep at 'The Vine' tonight."

"All right," replied Viv extremely lightly. "Pleasant dreams. Be good!"

Jimmie hung the receiver up thoughtfully. Again he was not thinking of the Murchison sighter. He was thinking what a beautiful figure Viv had. Then he pulled himself up short. That must be cut. He must not think of Viv—except as a partner in his schemes.

CHAPTER VIII

A DARING PLAN

Jimmie woke in his bedroom in "The Vine" public house. Snapping up the spring blind, he gazed earnestly across at the shuttered attic window of the *Coin de Paradis*, thirty yards distant. He wondered what Viv and Hyslop had found out last night in their daring reconnaissance of the hostile camp. Something important, he hoped; Viv was a clever girl. It was darn clever of her to have discovered that they were being followed and not to have given the show away by a slip at the end. He laughed as he thought of her and Hyslop playing Bezique for impossible stakes in a hotel of low repute near Leicester Square.

He turned away and dressed with care, slipping his automatic into his pocket as he finished. The discovery of the last day had warned him to be prepared for all emergencies. He was up against an unscrupulous combination with a master-brain at their head who would stop at little to get their prize safely over to Paris. At his request Hyslop, too, was now armed and so was Viv. Hyslop seemed thoroughly to enjoy a state of affairs, which to Jimmie was only repugnant. Clever tricking and the matching of cunning brain against cunning brain—yes, but brute force, wounding, or death—no.

His thoughts suddenly went off at a tangent. He had wandered over to the window again, and from where he stood he could just look down into the back yard of "The Vine." This dingy area, stacked with empty barrels and other rubbish, was much bigger than its neighbors, in fact, it stretched across the back premises of the first two houses in Warsaw Street. The result was that at its end it was only thirty feet from the back yard of the *Coin de Paradis*—thirty feet of a flat wall which a man might easily traverse. And Jimmie had also remembered that from the other and near end of "The Vine's" back yard a swing door led directly into Warsaw Street. He ruminated for a minute and finally stored the fact away in his mind.

A few minutes later he emerged from the private door of "The Vine" into Frith Street and immediately looked warily round. There was too much following going on, and though he was positive Number One's gang did not suspect him as yet, still he could not take risks. Let him make but one error, and they would realize they were being double-crossed. And then... Jimmie shivered as he thought of what would happen. They would not hesitate to put him out of the way.

* * * *

Soon after his arrival at the Grand Cross Hotel he was called on the telephone and found it was Inspector Gullidge speaking about the stiletto handle.

"That you, Rezaire?" he began. "Well, there was one passable finger-print."

"Good," answered Jimmie. "Whose?"

"Someone new, for we can't trace it anywhere in the records."

"Are you certain?" asked Jimmie incautiously.

"Of course I'm certain," snapped Gullidge. "I'm not an amateur like some people. A child could have traced it, because there's a peculiar, almost unique, scar on the ball of the right index. Shaped like a cross. If we can get a man with a scar like that on his right forefinger, it's all Scotland Yard to a village policeman he'll be the murderer."

"Right," said Jimmie sweetly. "I'll have him for you."

"Ho, will you?" he heard the Inspector snort to himself. Jimmie guessed how the man must be feeling, at seeing an ex-convict given a free hand on a detective's job, just because he had special information which he had refused to give up to the proper quarters.

"Bet you a level fiver I'll pull him before you?" he suggested airily.

Gullidge only snorted again and remarked icily: "Hold on and I'll connect you up with 'Captain Smith.' He wants you."

"Where is he speaking from?"

"Never you mind!" rapped out the Inspector, who was not in a good temper that morning. Jimmie grinned. When one has several thousand neatly docketed finger-prints of all criminals, including even pilferers, it is annoying to find a murderer's uncatalogued.

A moment later he heard 'Captain Smith's' voice. The interview was brief. 'Captain Smith' congratulated him on his find and then went on to say, with a hint of triumph, that he was afraid Jimmie wouldn't do much good in London. Awfully sorry, you know.

"Why?" asked Jimmie amazed.

"I happen to know you're working on a blind," returned 'Captain Smith.'

Jimmie had a strange suspicion. He himself had used the word "blind" in the faked notes that Neasden had found. Had Neasden passed the blind on?

"You mean," said Jimmie with a wild guess, "that you believe it's hidden elsewhere? Say, perhaps, somewhere on the East Coast?"

The momentary pause before 'Captain Smith' replied stiffly: "You leave my part of the show alone," showed that he had guessed right.

He jammed the receiver down at the end of the interview and rocked with laughter. Doubtless even now the redoubtable 'Captain Smith' was poring over the faked evidence which he, Rezaire, had manufactured and which Neasden, or the mysterious Number One, had probably cleverly passed on. He had set a trap for a fox; he had caught a whole pack of hounds as well. And he recalled now Neasden's reputed visit to Yarmouth yesterday. It was probable—no, certain—that when 'Captain Smith' made inquiries, if he had not done so already, there would be found near Yarmouth a launch chartered by a mysterious stranger for an unknown destination, and a few other false clues to keep the police busy. Well, that moved the Secret Service off the board; the battle was now between Number One and himself. He suddenly wondered how Number One had avoided the difficulty of the restaurant's name on the top of the menu card, and then realized that he would simply have torn it off. And—Rezaire suddenly slapped his leg—*that* would account for the changed handwriting on the menus on Sunday. Not even by the means of the handwriting on the card in his possession would 'Captain Smith' now be able to trace the restaurant concerned. Jimmie sobered as he realized what a subtle brain was this Number One, against whom he had so airily pitted himself.

He settled down in the lounge, impatiently waiting to hear what Viv would have to tell him. On her information he hoped that at last they might be able to work out some method of getting hold of the Murchison sighter and rounding up Number One and his gang. For time was getting on. There were only four days more.

* * * *

"Here you are!" said Jimmie at last. "Now let's have the story."

The three of them settled down at their usual corner table; for Jimmie always considered that a busy hotel lounge was the ideal place to discuss secrets and yet look innocent.

"I've had the most amazing luck," began Viv and paused for dramatic effect. "I've seen—or think I have—that Murchison bomb thing itself."

"Good God!" gasped Jimmie. "The devil you have! Are you certain?"

"Yes," interrupted Hyslop complacently, "on stirring up the jolly old brain, we've decided that Viv has seen the goods."

"I only had a second, but it's something like a small square frame-work of metal with levers that looked like a little metal ball with a hole in it. Oh, and I think there was a wire attached. Would that be it?"

"Sounds like it," said Jimmie excitedly. "Go on."

"Well"—Viv settled down happily for she loved a good story—"after H.H. and I staggered upstairs with our arms around each other's necks..."

"By the way, Viv, sorry to interrupt, but did you tip off that blonde? She's the girl I told you of, and she's one of the gang."

"Yes, I guessed that... Well, to resume. H.H lay down on a bed in a room above and looked green and I held his hand; and I'm damned if the old fat man didn't send up a waiter to watch us. However, he seemed soft, because when I vamped him and asked for a glass of water for H.H., who was letting off an occasional groan, he rushed downstairs to get it. At which I picked up my skirts and ran out..."

"Shouldn't have thought they'd have been in the way," grinned Jimmie.

"Now then, keep to business!" reproved Viv, but looked pleased nevertheless. "Well, I managed to give the whole place the rapid once-over. There were two other bedrooms on that floor, both looking innocent, so I skipped upstairs..."

"Good Lord!" groaned Jimmie seriously. "You might have ruined the whole show."

"The next floor," continued Viv, imperturbable in the knowledge of her success, "was practically the top, though a ladder led up further—probably to attics. In the back room I saw a light. So this child took a peep through the keyhole, and there I saw the contraption I've described on a table with a man evidently bending over it, for I could make out his hands."

"What devil's own luck!" murmured Rezaire.

"Wasn't it? But the fellow must have had a guilty conscience, because no sooner had I got this glimpse when he stopped, and came to the door. I had about a second to act—not time to get down the stairs. So I dodged into a room near by at the end of the passage and just shut the door in time. I heard him open his door,—it was locked, so he must have been doing something secret—and stand there listening. He hadn't seen me, and presently he went back."

"What did the man you saw look like?" inquired Rezaire.

"Small, clean-shaven, and I think a tooth or so missing in front. I couldn't look at him too closely."

"That's our laddie," said Hyslop. "The fellow who was with the blonde. We're getting quite a line on this Number One performin' troupe now, aren't we?"

"Wonder why he wasn't with the girl last night," Jimmie mused. "However, we now know for certain what we've suspected all along—that the Murchison sighter is kept in that restaurant. Back room on the third floor. You're certain they weren't suspicious of you?"

"I'm certain Viv and I weren't really suspected," put in Hyslop. "They put someone on to follow us, but that's because they're too darned efficient to take any chance. And we must jolly well have proved our innocence," he grinned.

"Or rather our guilt, H.H. By the way, you owe me seventeen thousand four hundred and sixty pounds."

"Now chuck fooling, you two. We've got to think. By the way," he added, struck with a thought, "I hope they don't keep it in a safe. If so it's going to be difficult. You say, Viv, that it wasn't on the table when you re-passed?"

"No. There was only a typewriter in a case. I *say*, I wonder…"

But Jimmie was on to it too. The word "Corona" in the dead man's shorthand which had so puzzled him suddenly fitted into the scheme with a click.

"That's it!" he cried, half to himself. "They'd be afraid of a safe, because it's so obvious, but mounted up instead of a typewriter with a locked cover over it… Keep quiet, you two! I've an idea!"

There was a silence while Jimmie thought rapidly. He had just remembered the back yard of "The Vine" and a vague plan had come to him. The chief requirement of any plan was swiftness in execution. A scheme which necessitated breaking open locks or a lengthy smuggling of the Murchison out of the building was not good, because there was the risk of being discovered before he had achieved his object. In which case no second chance would present itself, for the spies would take fright and change their intentions. His plan must be swift, simple, and above all, in the event of failure, must not be apparent as having been an attempt at all, in order that Number One and his gang might remain unsuspecting.

"Now listen," he began, when at last he saw his scheme stretching clearly before him in his mind. "This is what we are going to do; and we're going to do it tonight…"

* * * *

Half an hour later Jimmie ceased talking and straightened his back. "All quite clear now?" he added.

"Why not get the police in right at the start?" said Viv.

"Because, my dear, it's precious little credit in cash or anything we'll be allowed to retain by friend Gullidge if we do. Remember what I am and how I got the job and then guess what showdown I'll get if there's any dispute. No, we've got to get the thing ourselves and then have some flatties handy to round up the birds *when* we tell 'em where they are. Don't you agree, H.H.?"

"I think so. Though as far as I can see I shall jolly well need a dashed steel helmet for my part in the show."

"You'll be all right if you keep under cover. As for the Murchison it doesn't matter if it gets smashed. Our people don't necessarily want it intact—the idea is to get it away from this Number One and his gang."

"Look here, there's one thing. Supposing the game doesn't come off?"

"I've told you. I shall be quite the innocent guest at the restaurant, dining with my friend Neasden."

"Yes, old boy, you told me; but I mean, supposing they suspect you and don't let on that they have? They may try and dope your food? Poison in the jolly old nose-bag and so forth?" Rezaire thought rapidly. He remembered Mario and his tale of "the little white powder" in the coffee. If they did suspect, without doubt that was what would happen. He suddenly conceived a further daring line of attack under those circumstances; assuming he could rely upon Mario to give him warning, as he believed he could. It would be risking much, but it might turn previous failure into success.

With a few words he enlightened Hyslop, who sat back with amazement on his face. "They'll do you in, old lad," he said seriously.

Rezaire shook his head. "They'll only aim at putting me out of the way for a while and that's where you come in. You must be dining down below. I'll leave my overcoat downstairs to give me an excuse to signal to you if it's on. After that you must hang round to look after me in case I can't do it myself."

"It's madness," interposed Viv deliberately. "Think up something else, Jimmie boy!"

"No, my dear," he returned smiling. "The boldest way is always the best. And this should bear good fruit. During your criminal career have you ever noticed how careless people get in their speech in the presence of an unconscious man? Well, just imagine for once that the man wasn't really unconscious…"

* * * *

Viv pulled Jimmie's sleeve as he got up to go out with Hyslop on a reconnoitering expedition near "The Vine" for the evening's maneuver.

"Run away for a minute, H.H.!" she added. "I want to speak to Jimmie."

"Well?" said Rezaire when Hyslop had tactfully gone outside.

"Jimmie, I've got bad news."

"What?"

"When I got back to my flat last night, I found a note under the door."

"A note?"

"This." Viv drew a letter from her bag.

Rezaire took it and went white as he recognized the handwriting.

"Sam?" he exclaimed. "But he's—he's in the States?"

"Was," corrected the girl.

"But..."

She picked up a newspaper, turned a page and pointed to a paragraph. It referred to the recent theft of famous pictures from Lord Stamping's collection and stated that it was now established beyond doubt that this and a subsequent similar theft in Berkshire were the work of a gang of specialists from America.

"That's why he's over," said Viv.

"In that lot? But, damn it, he must be mad. I mean, if the police here catch him he'll take the nine o'clock walk to glory. He's wanted for the big thing."

"I know." The girl nodded soberly. "Read the note!"

"*Dear Viv*, (he read)

Didn't expect me did you? I'm going to drop in on a few old friends now I'm over. And it's no good going to the 'busy fellows' about me, because it'll only get you and others into trouble.

And I'm well hidden here. I'm going to come and see you at 11 A.M. tomorrow. Don't go trying a trap, because I shall know about it. I'm as clever now as any of the cowardly pikers you are so fond of.

With love, S."

"Well, I'm damned!" Jimmie was biting his lip as he felt his old terror sweeping back with overwhelming force, on realizing that Sam, his enemy, was actually in England. "The man must have been tight or mad when he wrote that. Why, we can tip him off to the police."

"No."

"No? Why not?"

"In the first place he must be well covered before he'd dare write that. And it doesn't tell the police anything; I bet they've heard he's over."

"But tomorrow?"

"He won't come if we try anything, and it'll only make him mad. Which'll be worse for me. I saw a fellow on watch outside my place this morning. He wasn't following me, just watching. A little fellow with a face like a white rat."

"Or a ferret?" asked Jimmie going pale.

"Yes."

"My God!" Rezaire was much disturbed. "He trailed *me* the other day. I didn't know he was Sam's jackal. Thank God I shook him off!"

He passed a hand across his forehead and found it wet.

"Viv!" he stammered. "Can you meet him tomorrow and tell him I'm not in London? For Heaven's sake don't give me away to him. Find out what he wants!"

"I know what he wants."

"What?"

"Me."

"You. But I thought…"

"Thought I'd given him the frozen shoulder in Paris. So I did. But he swore then he'd come back for me. He knows I'm not struck on him. He knows I'm…"

Jimmie suddenly remembered the last line of Sam's letter. Did it mean…? He looked at Viv and she dropped her eyes. Then his fear returned swamping all else:

"But Sam. I—I thought he was after *me*."

Viv looked at him queerly. "That's all part of it, Jimmie," she said steadily. "You must keep out of his way."

"You bet," replied Jimmie with feeling.

"I'll deal with him tomorrow," added the girl calmly.

Rezaire hesitated. He tried to think calmly. He knew Sam was not above trying to take what he wanted by force. He looked keenly at Viv, and saw suddenly that she was desperately afraid.

He swallowed once or twice; then with a dry throat muttered:

"Viv! Let me—Hyslop and me that is—be on hand in your flat tomorrow. Not so as Sam can see us, but hidden away—just in case you want help."

Viv stretched out a hand. She, better than anyone else, knew Jimmie's weakness and his terror of Sam; and she realized the sacrifice, as much as she desired it.

"All right," she agreed. "If everything we've planned for tonight is over satisfactorily by then, come to the back entrance of Shrewsbury Court by ten; and see you aren't spotted. Then I'll let you in and hide you… And—thank you, Jimmie," she finished simply.

Rezaire muttered something and left her to go after Hyslop. He felt a different man. All his self-confidence had oozed out of him, with the new and terrible knowledge that Sam was in London, Sam with his plotting for revenge and the evil knife he loved so well. He saw an enemy in every passer-by, and it was not till he had been listening some time to Hyslop's cheery burble that he partially regained his self-reliance and his interest in the coming night's work.

CHAPTER IX

AT GRIPS

Jimmie Rezaire, a furtive crouching figure on the roof beside the *Coin de Paradis* window, was peering intently over the parapet into the darkness beneath. By the aid of Hyslop's little steel tool with the teeth that gripped the bolts and moved them a fraction of an inch each time, he had some while ago finished his skillful manipulation of the attic shutters, and the upper portion of the *Coin de Paradis* now lay open to him whenever he chose to enter. But he was waiting for a signal from Hyslop hidden below on the far side of the wall which enclosed the back premises of the restaurant; and Hyslop was watching a lighted window just below the attic which showed that there was still someone inside the room with the stolen Murchison sighter.

Jimmie shifted his position restlessly and cursed to himself. It was getting late. If he didn't hear from Hyslop soon, he would have himself to signal that he was going in in spite of the light in the room below, though for the smoothest working of his plan, he wanted that room to be empty.

Even as he moved, the awaited signal came—the faint red glow of a torch covered over by a human hand. It shone dimly thrice, and Jimmie repeated it once in answer. In another moment he had clambered over the sill and had disappeared inside the attic as noiselessly as a shadow.

His feet touched bare boards and there was a smell of emptiness. He had expected that the attic would be unoccupied, but he moved with infinite caution to avoid knocking over any lumber. His outstretched fingers soon touched a wall which he followed to a door. Here he paused to satisfy himself there was no one outside and then switched on his torch.

It shone on a bare sloping-roofed apartment, empty except for some piled boxes and a roll or two of carpet; but Jimmie's first care was to re-bolt the shutters and remove all traces of his entry, even examining the floor to make certain the dusty surface did not show footmarks. Then he stole to the door. Though it was locked, a bare moment's work with a businesslike skeleton key saw him peeping cautiously through into another and larger attic, sparsely furnished and with two camp-beds. In the near corner was a trap-door in the floor, the only means of egress. After relocking the door behind him, Jimmie switched off his torch and tested the trap-door, to find that luckily it was not fastened. He raised it sufficiently to look through.

For about half a minute he stared into the lighted passage beneath him, fixing all the details in his mind, for he would need them later. Leading down from the trap-door was the ladder Viv had mentioned; near its foot was the door to the back room and beyond this the door to the lavatory and the staircase leading further downward. From below came the sounds of the restaurant in full swing, the clatter of plates, and an occasional order shouted in French, while the hot smell of cooking hung against the ceiling and streamed up past his face through the opening.

Silently Jimmie opened the trap-door to its full extent and drew from his pocket a queer tool like a small metal bar held at the end by a rubber grip. This he laid beside him and, stretching an arm downward, he just managed to reach the socket of the electric light that hung by a cord from the ceiling close by and illuminated the landing. Pulling it in to him, he cast a last swift glance round to impress the scene finally on his memory; then he detached the globe and laid it beside him, thus leaving the upper floor in darkness. The socket he retained in his hand.

Everything had been done with skill and rapidity; indeed, barely five minutes had passed since he entered the attic. He wondered if Hyslop were ready too, down below in the back yard, where a cautious reconnoitering expedition during the slack hours that afternoon had revealed an unused electric socket accessible through a scullery window. He altered his position to one of greater readiness; from now on he would have to move very, very swiftly.

"Here goes!" he muttered and with a quick decisive movement he picked up the rubber-insulated tool beside him and jammed the metal bar across the two bared points of the globeless fixture.

A bright blue flash leaped under the touch and he saw the lights disappear in the two floors below as the fuses blew. Only a gleam from the restaurant floor persisted; then that too went, as Hyslop, waiting similarly equipped in his position below, managed the lower part of the house equally efficiently on seeing Rezaire's success. Before the outbreak of protest and surprise from the diners had died down, Jimmie had replaced the globe, letting it swing back uselessly on its cord, closed the trap-door, and was at the foot of the attic ladder.

"Well done, H.H.!" he was thinking to himself, as he noiselessly and unerringly made his way towards the back room. He tried the door; then his fingers moved swiftly among his keys. There was now only a single lock keeping him from the tin case pretending so innocently to contain a Corona typewriter—only a door between him and the Murchison sighter.

Success was a matter of bare minutes. A few steps, perhaps a brief search, and the Murchison sighter would drop from the window into the yard beneath, to be gathered up quickly by Hyslop, once more crouching under the cover of the wall. Thence a casual cask among the empties in "The Vine's" back yard would receive its remains and the secret would be safe. Immediately after this, a signal of success would go, via the swing-door to the yard, from Hyslop to Viv expectant at a telephone, and from her to a sceptical though waiting inspector at the nearest police-station. Before the spies could know they were even suspected, they would have been rounded up.

But this final half of the plan was conditional on success in the former. If Jimmie did not obtain the sighter this time, he did not want the police to learn anything which would give them a chance to interfere and spoil his future chances. Further still, he did not want the spies to know that an attempt had even been made. Hence his re-bolting of the shutters and all the precautions he had taken over the fusing of the lights; hence, too, the peculiar fact that he was wearing an overcoat over a dinner jacket, and was without a hat.

And there was only a door between...

The first and second keys failed, but Jimmie had two more, one of which he knew would do it.

At that moment the door of the other room along the passage opened, though no light showed.

Jimmie heard someone come out and begin to feel his way along the landing. He came nearer, the sound of his breathing was distinct in the darkness. A few feet away he stopped and called over the banisters in a low voice: "Mario! Mario!"

A sudden thrill of terror ran through Jimmie and the keys almost dropped from his fingers; for the voice was that of the little man with the moustache who had run out of Jewel Court that Friday night, the possessor of the scar on the forefinger—the murderer of the Secret Service agent.

For a moment Jimmie hesitated, his heart thumping wildly. He dared not move with this man almost at his elbow. At the mere thought his ribs began to tingle as though he already felt a steel blade. Yet he dared not wait while the other stood there; for very soon the fuses would be repaired. He had allowed for about five minutes' darkness at the most: if he was caught in the light it would mean failure, without a second chance—if not death.

At that instant the little man moved onward towards the head of the stairs apparently intending to go down himself. Just in time Jimmie pressed himself close against that tantalizingly locked door; and the other safely passed without touching him.

Jimmie thought rapidly. The situation was worse. He still could not renew his attempt on the door; yet it was increasingly risky to wait. The only thing left to do was to give up hope of success on this occasion and concentrate on the second part of his plan—the avoidance of suspicion by getting down to the restaurant floor. On the other hand, the little man had by his movement now nearly barred Jimmie from this preconceived method of extrication.

Noiselessly he tiptoed to the head of the stairs where the other man, after pausing again to call softly for Mario to bring a candle, had started to descend. Jimmie softly followed.

On the landing below Jimmie was still at the murderer's heels. There was only one flight more to the upper room of the restaurant. In the depths of the basement he thought he could see the first flicker of a candle. Thank Heaven in a metropolis which depended so entirely on electric light, candles were generally stored away inaccessibly. But the little man had stopped again. It must be now or never. Holding his coat close to him Jimmie stepped silently and swiftly past, locating his enemy by the breathing.

As ill luck had it the man turned. His coat brushed Jimmie.

"Is anyone there?" he said in a surprised voice.

Jimmie was now past—at the top of the stairs.

"Who's that?" repeated the voice sharply.

Jimmie tried a gigantic bluff. A vision of the fat Monsieur Villon with his "*Que voulez vous*" flashed into his mind.

"*Que voulez vous?*" he puffed in a mumbled undertone, and was delighted to find how at the first trial he had so accurately hit off the fat old man's tone. He grunted and ponderously descended the stairs. He was praying desperately that the man above might not suspect, might not bother to ask what the proprietor was doing up there. Luckily he had not a torch, Jimmie knew—or he would have used it when he first came out of his room.

To his immense relief there was no further reply from above beyond a muttered grumble at the absence of light. Jimmie pursued his way down, controlling his anxious feet to Monsieur Villon's normal pace. In the basement he could now distinctly see harassed waiters starting up with candles. The customers were chattering in the dark restaurant, accepting the situation with laughter.

He stripped off his coat; as he reached the outside of the upper room someone who sounded like a waiter bumped into him and said "*Pardon!*"

The voices of the diners on the ground floor grew quite plain as Jimmie, slipping swiftly downward, hung his coat on some pegs he had located just inside the doorway of the lower room.

Then he gave a deep sigh of relief—the first real breath that he had taken since he swung open the attic shutters. And that was a bare ten minutes ago, though it had seemed like an hour.

A waiter carrying a tray of lighted candles appeared from below and turned into the restaurant. A moment later the lights were switched on again at the main, the fuses having been replaced. The waiter with the candles turned back, his curse inaudible in the cheer that went up from the diners.

The clatter of knives and forks was resumed as the lights blazed. Jimmie Rezaire, an innocent figure in a dinner jacket, was disclosed, about to mount the steps to the first-floor room. A puzzled look was on his face as if in wonder at the absence of light upon his arrival from outside. He even stopped a passing waiter and asked what had happened.

As Jimmie leisurely mounted, Neasden appeared from the upper room and called in a low but angry tone to the man out of sight upstairs. Then he turned round and saw Jimmie. Rezaire noticed that he looked annoyed at being thus seen talking to his companion above. Then:

"Good evening," he said pleasantly. "Here you are!"

"Afraid I'm a little late," apologized Rezaire, coolly master of the situation once more. "And the whole place was in darkness when I arrived."

"The lights blew out, I understand. What have you done to your knee?"

"Fell on the stairs just now," lied Jimmie, brushing off dust from where he had knelt by the trap-door. As he spoke, he was straining his ears for any sudden sound from upstairs denoting discovery of some clue to his attempt. None came, and he breathed more easily. After all, he was safe enough; he had replaced everything exactly as it had been; there was nothing to give him away; and he had bluffed his way out of the only difficult situation which had arisen. But it had been touch and go. He hoped, as he entered the room behind Neasden, that the little man upstairs would not remember to mention the incident to the proprietor. But even if he did, they would not necessarily suspect him.

Once again the upper room was empty of customers except for the girl, whom Mario was helping to a dish. Jimmie began to realize that that upper room was carefully guarded indeed and that the general public were in reality denied access except when, like Hyslop, they knew of its existence and forced a way up. Yet Number One was clever enough not to close it completely; nominally it was open to anyone and so above suspicion.

To his surprise Neasden at once took Jimmie over to the girl's table, and motioning Mario away, introduced them with a smile.

"This is Zita—one of our happy family."

"I had no idea," lied Jimmie as one amazed.

"We have spoken together," said the girl smiling at him. "By Number One's orders."

Jimmie managed to look even more astounded, though this remark only confirmed his previous suspicion, that his conversation with the girl Zita had been deliberately planned to test his secretiveness.

"And you scored badly off her," laughed Neasden. "Police officer you said you were, didn't you? Number One was so amused."

"Well, since I'm not to see him, I'm glad I've amused him," replied Jimmie, angling for further information.

Neasden, however, turned it off by leading him back to another table, the very one where Hyslop and Viv had sat the night before.

"A good girl, Zita," he confided to Jimmie. "Most useful to us…"

He stopped, as Mario reentered with a menu-card, and ordered a meal with care. Jimmie studied him with a new interest. It was the first time he had sat face to face with Neasden knowing him to be one of the spies he was after. He would need all his wits, this time.

"Now," began the big man, when they had started, "I'm afraid I've treated you rather badly so far; but I've been extremely busy lately. I think I told you when last we met that my talk of burglary and so on was a blind. Have you any idea what our real game is?"

For a moment Jimmie was tempted to shake his head. Then he remembered that he was up against clever people who knew, moreover, that he himself was no fool. To make himself out dense, therefore, would be to court suspicion. And Number One,—he remembered with a shiver—had drastic methods with traitors.

"I have a suspicion," he said deliberately. "If instead of pictures and collectors you had talked of, say, military secrets and foreign governments you would have been nearer truth?"

"Exactly," purred Neasden. "We specialize in obtaining any information required and in supplying it to those who commission us. In order to avoid suspicion, therefore, and continue safely in business, we have to lay our plans with great care. Have you noticed how often detection of crime is due to lack of forethought in the original plan, not lack of care in execution? Brains always tell. Our Number One is of course the master-mind, but we others have to be of a high standard, hence our desire to secure you!"

Jimmie bowed ironically and wondered to himself what to take next. So far he had merely concentrated on extricating himself without suspicion from his unsuccessful attempt on the Murchison; he had not yet turned his mind to the future. For the moment he was without a plan, but perceived that the best thing to do was to let events take their present course. He might thus learn something of value from Neasden himself.

"Well," he began briskly, "it's nice of you to say all this, but the question now is: what do you want me to do? My—er—brain is at your service."

"We are just concluding a piece of business—or rather by next Friday we shall have done." Jimmie easily read the Murchison sighter into this. "Our next order is from the same third party, a client who is now interested in tanks. There is a new type of tank-track in existence—secret at present. Number One has worked out a rough scheme of operations and you and I are to carry it out in our own way and with such additions and suggestions…"

He paused again as Mario appeared with their next course.

Jimmie sat in silence, deeply disappointed.

He had hoped he was about to obtain fuller information about the spies' plans for the Murchison, and now realized he was not to be let into that secret at all. He didn't care a rap about new tank-tracks or the future activities of the Number One Performing Troupe, as the irrepressible Hyslop had nicknamed them. Indeed, if he pulled his job off, there would not be a Number One or a troupe at all by the time his help was required in this new matter.

Soon Mario left them once more and Neasden resumed his conversation. He was acting obviously on instructions from Number One.

Suddenly Mario reentered in haste and gave Neasden a folded square of paper.

Jimmie, affecting not to look, tried hard to read its contents, but the writing was small and close and he could not make out a word. Evidently, however, it was important, for Neasden rose.

"You will excuse me one moment?" he asked as he left the room.

Rezaire for some reason felt apprehensive. Why had Neasden been called out? Perhaps something had been discovered about his entry. No, he was a fool to let himself get rattled like this. If he had left any clue to his movements, he would have learned about it by now. Besides he was certain he had done everything exactly as he and Hyslop and Viv had planned. He wondered suddenly if that note had been from Number One.

Neasden returned. His face with its enormous nose, which amused Hyslop so much, looked as impassive as ever. He sat down and, as if their previous subject had been disposed of, asked Jimmie some question about his adventures.

Jimmie read a dangerous significance into this. The other had relinquished the subject of the tank-track. If so, it could only mean that they had suddenly grown suspicious. Something had happened to make them so, during the minute Neasden had been absent. He answered perfunctorily and then said: "Well, carry on with the idea!"

"Shall we leave it till after coffee?" suggested Neasden carelessly. "That waiter continually coming in and out worries me."

"Certainly," said Jimmie lightly, though he felt the matter was now serious. Obviously it had just been decided—perhaps by Number One—that Jimmie was not to be told anything more till suspicion had been cleared from him. But what had they found out; and how?

"Did you go upstairs when you came here tonight?" asked Neasden abruptly, staring straight at him.

"Upstairs?" Jimmie looked slightly puzzled.

"Yes, to the floor above."

"Oh, that!" Rezaire realized that the other must have had something to go upon, and that blank denial would be dangerous. "I missed this door in the dark and went up a few steps too far. I ran into the proprietor—what's his name? Villon—coming down, and he put me right."

"Oh, I see," said Neasden and was silent again.

"Why did you ask?" pursued Jimmie casually.

"No particular reason. I thought I heard your footsteps."

Jimmie knew the other was lying, but he hoped he himself had been believed. He thought he had bluffed quite well, lending color as well to his impersonation of the proprietor.

Neasden stretched his long arms, looking huger than ever.

"What about coffee now, eh?"

"That'll suit me fine."

"Then we'll go into Number One's instructions in comfort."

The coffee soon came and Mario poured it out for them. Then he stood over Rezaire with the sugar basin and asked politely:

"Two spoonsful, sair?"

Not a muscle of Jimmie's face quivered as he heard this, his prearranged warning from Mario. "Thanks," he replied quietly. He felt that a load of uncertainty was off his mind. He realized now that at any rate, though he did not know what had led them to it, they suspected him enough to want him doped for a while.

He stirred the coffee that, though holding the "little white powder," looked so innocent, and deliberated. Now at last was the opportunity to put into action the further audacious plan he had worked out with Hyslop that morning for just such a situation as this. It would mean putting himself into the power of the spies, and if they discovered he was acting for the Secret Service…well good-bye. But he was positive they could not guess that yet; for was he not Rezaire the ex-convict?

Anyhow, it was worth the risk, and might mean success. As he had told Viv, people were apt to be careless in their speech in the presence of an unconscious man. And Hyslop would be at hand.

He rose, noting with secret joy Neasden's sudden discomfiture.

"Just going to get a cigar from my overcoat pocket down below," he remarked carelessly. "I'm dying for one."

"Have one of mine!" offered the big man eagerly. "Save you a journey!"

"No, thanks." Rezaire could not resist a dig. "It's not as bad as all that."

He left the baffled spy wondering furiously if Jimmie had suddenly grown wary.

CHAPTER X

COFFEE AND AFTER

Jimmie passed quickly down the stairs to the restaurant. The cheerful noise of ordinary people dining and chattering without a thought of spies in their heads, attracted him strongly. For a moment he was tempted to call off his dangerous scheme and walk out into the street, free and safe.

But that would be madness in reality. At the moment he believed that Number One could only suspect him of vague interference in what didn't concern him. If he ran away guiltily, he would show himself as a traitor; in which case he would not be free and safe for long.

As he reached his coat, hung by the restaurant door, he cast a quick glance over the diners. A few feet away and facing him was Hyslop, a vacuous expression on his countenance as he ate beefsteak. Instantly Jimmie felt better. Everything was ready. Hyslop, after realizing the attempt had been unsuccessful, had signalled the news to Viv and had then hurried round here to be on hand if required. Viv's part was over and she had no doubt now gone back to her flat, after telephoning to the police-inspector that he would not be required—another small triumph for Gullidge's jealousy.

Jimmie fumbled in his overcoat and extracted first a case of cigars left there for this very excuse, and secondly a tiny but highly absorbent sponge, just of the right size to be held unnoticed in the mouth. Next he deftly slipped into the overcoat pocket his torch and the few tools he had used in carrying out his earlier plan, also his revolver. These would give him away if he was searched; and so he had arranged for Hyslop to remove them shortly afterwards, while getting his own coat. During all this he kept a wary eye about him to see that Monsieur Villon was not watching, for Monsieur Villon, though not one of the gang itself, was employed by them and no doubt in their pay. But Monsieur Villon was not visible; Jimmie had not seen him all the evening.

Satisfied that Hyslop was now warned of his intention, he went upstairs again, to find Neasden obviously pleased to see him again. It was evident he had been on tenter-hooks lest Jimmie had suspected what was prepared for him and had run away.

"It's always in the last pocket," grumbled Jimmie to explain his delay.

"That's so. Your coffee's getting cold."

"Oh, thanks."

Jimmie carelessly lifted the cup. He could feel Neasden's intentness, though the big man, well trained, made no outward sign. There was a breathless stillness behind him, too, and Rezaire realized that in his absence Zita had been told of his intended drugging.

With the cup half-way to his lips, Jimmie was overtaken by a sneeze, and the coffee trembled perilously in mid-air. This he was delighted to see broke Neasden's assumed composure for a second. Momentarily the spy made as if to snatch the cup to safety, but restrained himself and critically examined his cigar instead.

"Nasty cold!" he obviously forced himself to murmur.

"Haven't I?" agreed Jimmie cheerfully. He had replaced the cup and was fumbling for an enormous handkerchief, with which he enveloped his face to repair the ravages of the sneeze.

Then without a further word he picked up the little coffee cup and drained it in a gulp. He heard a faint sigh of relief from Zita, apparently more highly strung than Neasden.

Quickly Jimmie picked up his cigar lying ready, and inserting it into his lips struck a match and drew with absorbing deliberation. To Neasden he probably appeared absurdly careful over this; but Jimmie was experiencing difficulty in lighting his cigar at all with his mouth filled by a little sponge into which the contents of a small cup of coffee had just been poured. Both this and the cigar he was now trying to manipulate as naturally as possible without squeezing any of the drugged coffee down his throat.

"Have a brandy!" offered Neasden as soon as the cigar was alight.

Jimmie nodded; he could not speak. At that instant his cigar fell from his lips to the floor. He bent down after it, opened his mouth wide the moment his head was below the table and let the coffee-sodden sponge drop out. As he reappeared with his cigar, he kicked the sponge under the radiator. After which he thanked Neasden and said, with much truth, that a little brandy would do him good.

When the little glass arrived, Jimmie took a chance on its not having been tampered with as well and drank to his own cleverness. His actions throughout had been so quick and skillful that neither Zita nor Neasden could possibly have suspected he had not swallowed the drug. He began to wonder how soon the powder normally took effect, because he now had to play his part—a part which he hoped would put him in possession of much valuable information and would eventually bring him success.

* * * *

After five minutes of desultory conversation, in which Neasden was careful not to give away any further information about Number One or his subordinates, Rezaire was suddenly assailed with a strange swimming in his head. For a moment he thought his ruse had failed and that he had been drugged by other means than the coffee. Then he realized that it was simply the effect of the small amount of coffee that had of necessity stayed in his mouth after ejecting the sponge. It gave him his cue and he at once leaned his head on his hand, making out that he felt worse than he was.

Neasden triumphantly bent across to him:

"What's the matter?"

"Not very well," mumbled Jimmie convincingly.

"Had too much to drink?" suggested Neasden pleasantly, and as Jimmie bent further forward with half-closed eyes, whipped up from under the table a second empty wine-bottle. At the same time he deftly changed coffee cups. Jimmie slumping artistically in his chair nearly opened his eyes in amazement at the man's foresight. Secure though they were in that upper room, yet had by any chance even a police officer walked in, there was nothing to show that Jimmie's coffee had been drugged and there was everything, even down to Zita's independent evidence, to prove that Jimmie was fuddled with alcohol.

He allowed himself to be lifted to his feet, conscious that the girl was helping. Neasden, still playing his part, was murmuring little sentences about the wine being strong and a nice rest being all he wanted. They started to assist him from the room; and Jimmie took care to throw his full weight on Neasden's arm. Zita's hands fluttered over his pockets and he heard her breathe "No gun" to her partner.

Though he made no move to help himself he was carried very quickly upstairs. He kept his eyes closed, he could risk nothing at this juncture; for by now he was probably supposed to be quite unconscious. Besides, the small trace of coffee he had not been able to avoid had made him genuinely dizzy, but this he knew would soon pass off.

He was carried into a back room, the one underneath that in which the Murchison sighter was hidden. Here he was laid on the floor in a corner.

"Too easy!" he heard Neasden say in curt triumphant tones. "Took it like a little lamb."

"Poor fish!" answered Zita contemptuously.

"See what he's got on him!" ordered Neasden. "We may be able to make out his game."

"Not me," retorted the girl. "I'm not going to kneel down in a good dress. Do it yourself!" Neasden knelt beside him. Either he had great faith in or great experience with the drug for, beyond casually lifting Jimmie's wrist for a second, he did not bother to examine him at all, but simply went through his pockets. There was nothing there of any value; Jimmie had of course been prepared. By now, too, Hyslop would have seen that his overcoat was equally innocent, if they thought of examining that.

"Nothing," grunted the big man getting to his feet. "Still I suppose we've done right."

There was a silence. Jimmie guessed that Neasden was standing looking down at him, and at once experienced an overpowering longing to open his eyes. To do so would be fatal, yet the longing grew and grew. In another moment he felt he would have ruined everything by yielding to this irrational obsession, when he heard Neasden turn away with a laugh.

"Queer face he's got!"

"It gives me the creeps. Clever-looking chap, though."

"You're getting a mass of nerves, Zita."

"Put the bag over his head," he heard Zita say. "I keep feeling he's going to open his eyes and look at me. If he does I shall scream. You're certain he's not shamming?"

"Pah! He got his shot all right. Gulped the lot in front of my eyes. And if you scream I'll wring your pretty neck. However, I'll do it!" Jimmie's head was lifted and a bag of soft black material was quickly drawn over it. Believing for an instant he was about to be suffocated, he nearly leaped to his feet; then common sense came to his aid as he realized that had that been the intention they would not have spoken about it as they had. The bag was loosely knotted under his chin; and there was plenty of space for fresh air to get past. Jimmie found himself free to open his eyes at last, but to his dismay found he could not hear nearly so well.

As Neasden got to his feet, Zita said: "Better tell Davis that we've got him, hadn't you, Roman?" To which the man answered with something Jimmie's ear could not catch and Zita, whose voice penetrated better, replied: "I suppose Number One will ring up about him soon." Then he heard the door shut behind Neasden who, whatever his real name, was evidently called "Roman." Visualizing his nose, Rezaire guessed why.

Jimmie lay motionless, his head in the hot darkness of the bag. So far his plan had gone well. The slight effects of the drug had worn off and his brain was clear. He began to consider what he had already learned. Number One was not in the *Coin de Paradis* then this night. Perhaps he did not live there at all, but communicated by telephone or arranged meetings, being too wise to frequent the same place as his subordinates. And Number One was expected to ring up soon with instructions as to his disposal. Again he hoped fervently Number One had no grounds for thinking he had anything to do with the Secret Service. Then there was the man referred to as Davis. Davis must be the chap whom he had encountered above—the murderer, with the scar on the forefinger...

Neasden had reentered the room with Davis. Jimmie had been right; he recognized the newcomer's voice in his greeting to Zita.

He strained every nerve to try and follow what was said.

"Good work, Davis!" remarked Zita and then, woman-like, asked several questions at once. "What was he trying to do? How did you spot him? I thought he was practically fixed up with us?"

"So he was; practically," put in Neasden. "If I hadn't been sent off to Yarmouth by Number One yesterday, he would have been. As it is, he knows something."

"Not about the machine, surely?"

Jimmie guessed at once that the machine was their name for the Murchison sighter.

"Not a word as far as I know."

"Thank God!" said the girl.

"But I must say," put in Davis, "that's what I thought he was nosing after. It was him up above in the dark, Zita, I'll swear. I touched someone and spoke, and the figure said '*Que voulez vous.*' For a moment I passed it over, and then I suddenly realized that of course it was impossible. So I sent a note, warning Roman. Then I got Number One on the phone about it and he was worried, I can tell you."

Neasden laughed. "He was still worried when I came out and spoke to him and he told me to make sure there wasn't an explanation. So when I came back I asked this bird of ours a test question or two and he admitted, clever devil, that he had been up a little way; but he spoiled it by adding he had run into the proprietor! As *I* knew there wasn't a proprietor here tonight, he was caught out."

Jimmie, who had been able to make out most of the talk, swore silently to himself at this. He perceived now how his clever impersonation at that risky moment had been completely nullified by the fact that Monsieur Villon was apparently not in the restaurant at all that evening. For once his amazing luck had deserted him.

Neasden was saying something Jimmie could not hear and Davis answered: "Beats me what his game is. He can't possibly be a 'busy'; or even a 'nose.'"

At that moment a telephone bell, muted to a discreet buzz, broke out. Number One, thought Jimmie, with a sense of small triumph. At least the mysterious Number One's voice was now sounding in the same room as himself. He was at any rate nearer the unapproachable.

"Right," he heard Zita say and added something that was evidently a password. Then: "Roman, he wants you!"

"Hullo," said Neasden. "Yes, Davis was right… We've got him up here… Yes, he's fast asleep… No, we can't make it out, nothing on him. What…? Davis"—he broke off—"Number One asks was there any trace of entry above?"

"Nothing. I had a look at once."

Neasden repeated this over the wire. "No, I can't see a reason. He can't know about the machine. Maybe sheer curiosity… Yes… Except that he's not speaking the truth somewhere. Something fishy. Clever chap, I know… Fresh instructions? Right, I'm listening…"

There came a long sentence, broken only by an occasional "Yes" or "Right" from Neasden. Jimmie, an adept in intrigue, was at first amazed that Number One thus appeared to talk so openly over the phone, when, for all he knew, the police might have planted a listener at the exchange for calls to and from the *Coin de Paradis*. Then he realized that it was not so foolish after all. Too much secrecy defeated its own ends and merely aroused suspicion where none was. The astute Number One had no reason to suppose that his activities at M. Villon's well-known restaurant were even guessed at; indeed, such opponents as were interested in him were probably now away watching mystery motor-boats at Yarmouth.

He heard the receiver go down and Neasden ask something in an undertone, to which Davis, after first opening the door, answered: "No one. All safe!"

Then Neasden began to speak in such a low voice that in spite of his efforts Jimmie could not make out all the words. Nevertheless he strained every nerve to follow the general sense; for the very first sentence he heard told him of the extreme importance of the conversation that was going on. It proved the success of his well-planned ruse. It proved, too, as he had said to Viv, that even the cleverest plotters can yet be so careless as to talk in the presence of an unconscious man, without making absolutely certain he is as unconscious as they think. For what Neasden was telling the other two was nothing more nor less than an alteration in Number One's plans for getting the Murchison sighter over to France.

CHAPTER XI

A NIGHT DRIVE

Number One, Jimmie thankfully gathered from Neasden's half-heard sentences, had decided not to suspect him of treachery. His previous record of crime had saved him for the time being, though he was to be sent away that night and kept quiet at an unknown place called "The Gables." Later on an explanation would be required; and if then he turned out to be double-crossing—here he shivered with a sudden terror—he was to be put out. Neasden mentioned it as calmly as if he was talking of killing a puppy.

But Number One had evidently been disturbed by the incident. He had decided,—and this was the information which delighted Jimmie and set his brain buzzing with schemes to get free—to set forward his arrangements. Other factors, too, had apparently brought up this decision. The mysterious Siminski had cabled that he was coming earlier, by airplane, and would arrive in Paris tomorrow evening to stay at "the usual hotel," and there was something, too, about "François at Calais." In short, the "machine" was to go over in two days' time—on Wednesday the 17th, instead of the 19th.

Though rejoicing at having learned of this vital change, Jimmie nevertheless realized that it made time more valuable than ever. The eleven A.M. train from Victoria Station on Wednesday was apparently the one selected, owing to some prearranged plan with a Calais Customs official; so he only had thirty-six hours. And he was to be a prisoner, he gathered, till it was too late. Could he make his escape? And could he defeat them successfully in the time...?

His thought was interrupted by someone picking him up.

"Well," Neasden was saying, "better get this chap over to 'The Gables.' Doesn't look as though he'd be one of us now after all. Anyway, I'm glad Number One's so certain he's not a nose."

"Personally, I think we ought to bump him off," said Davis.

"Oh, you're just jumpy because you ran into him the night you did in the police spy," said Zita contemptuously. "That was sheer chance. I agree with Number One; we can't go putting people out because they walk too far in the dark."

"Anyhow, wait till the machine's disposed of," added Neasden. "We can judge him then."

They now had Jimmie upright and were wrapping him round and round with some thick material which felt like carpet. Dust came out of it and Jimmie, after a heroic struggle, decided that unconscious men were not permitted to sneeze. After he had been roped round, he was taken outside and left in the passage. It was only with extreme difficulty that he could now make out what was said, but he thought he heard Davis say he was going to get Lew round with the car.

Jimmie lay there for a long period of time, blind and half-suffocated, hearing only the vibration of traffic or Neasden's heavy footfalls in the next room. He felt like an inanimate parcel packed and labelled and merely awaiting the delivery van for "The Gables." He tried to concentrate his thoughts on what he had overheard of Number One's orders, translated through Neasden to the other spies, till he was interrupted by two men coming upstairs. They picked him up roughly by head and feet and carried him down. Though he was being taken to an unknown destination and was in the hands of men who would not hesitate to kill him if they suspected his real aim, Jimmie was fairly calm. The thought of Hyslop comforted him. In fact, his chief fear at the time was lest they should bang his head against a wall.

He reached the ground-floor. The restaurant was silent, evidently closed for the night. Once he heard Mario's voice in whining expostulation and Neasden roughly telling him to hold his tongue. He realized that it was not only his threat of exposure that had allied Mario to him, but the little man's detestation of those whom he had to serve. Poor Mario—a non-combatant between two opposing forces, bound to get it in the neck somewhere. Jimmie felt quite sorry for the little waiter.

He was out in the street and heard an automobile engine. An onlooker would merely have seen two men loading a roll of carpet into a truck. Jimmie fervently hoped Hyslop was somewhere on watch; otherwise he would be badly landed. He hoped, too, that Hyslop would have the sense to see through the trick, for he felt there were similar rolls of carpet in the van with him. Only thirty-six hours left; and there was quite a chance he might spend them a prisoner with all his valuable information rendered useless!

He heard Davis saying something to the van driver, Lew, about "being all right till next morning"—which he took to refer to himself. He heard, and smiled grimly, the unmistakable footfall of a policeman. Then the machine started up and he was off.

* * * *

Jimmie kept his sense of direction sufficiently to realize that the general trend was to the north, as the truck sped onward. He soon ascertained, too, that, though there were two men on the driver's seat, there was no one inside, and so he took the opportunity of twisting himself about as much as possible; for he was very stiff from long inaction.

They went on and on. They came into an area of trams and passed it. Traffic noises died away, and at last Rezaire judged they were in the open country. To the north of London too, he now knew for certain; because once they stopped and he heard the driver ask for the Stevenage road. The answer was lost to Jimmie's ears, but he guessed they must be near Hatfield where the main road forked. He was appalled at the mention of Stevenage. Where were they taking him? Hyslop would never find him. He had been a fool to trust the fellow so completely. Though the lad was clever, he was very inexperienced.

Driven by this fear he began to try and free himself. His hands were not tied, but he was rolled up like a cocoon in a length of carpet which itself was tied outside. Also he was half stifled by the bag over his head. He found his arms were useless; and at last tried to wriggle his body upward right through the imprisoning cylinder.

In a quarter of an hour he had his head out, but he was feeling nearly dead. Another ten minutes and he had worked his shoulders well over and got one arm free. After which it was easy to undo the bag, and finally untie the cords round the carpet.

Taking deep breaths of the cold night air, he sat a free but battered man on the floor of the van, and pondered. The situation was not attractive. He was miles out in the country, he had probably been lost by his companion and he was in a dinner-jacket. Also he was unarmed and his two captors probably were not.

At that moment, with a shriek of a horn, a car overtook them and passed at great speed. A minute later the truck braked, the driver shouting angrily to someone in front. Peeping through the window ahead, Jimmie saw the car that had just passed halted with its nose in the ditch as though it had skidded. Its body blocked the road, the reason for the driver's anger.

In spite of his protests, his van was forced to a standstill and Jimmie could have shouted with joy as he heard, incredibly in that deserted countryside, Hyslop's voice, amiably fatuous.

"Frightfully sorry, old lads, but I've had a beastly rotten skid…"

"Well, drive off the bloody road then!"

"Can't. My jolly old engine has…"

"Get off the road!" flamed the second man and dismounted. He looked like a prize-fighter, as he stepped threateningly into the circle of light from his lamps.

"I keep telling you, old love, I can't move it. You'll both have to give a hand and shove." Jimmie, wondering what Hyslop's plan was, buttoned his coat over his shirt front and slipped silently out of the back of the truck. The two men were both now in the light, grumbling angrily, but prepared to help move the obstruction to their passage; when suddenly Hyslop snapped out: "Hands up!"

An automatic shone in his fist; his voice had lost its fatuity.

"Well, I'm—" began the prize-fighter.

"You aren't yet, but you darn soon will be, if you don't put 'em up!" flashed Hyslop. "I know you're thinking of making a rush and if you do I'll plug you in the guts."

Jimmie smiled as the young man thus forestalled the other's action. That particular threat always made an assailant hesitate. Two pairs of hands went up reluctantly.

Hyslop's next problem, how to keep two men quiet while he freed his companion, was solved by Jimmie himself who stepped forward quickly behind them and ran his hands over their pockets, producing two guns. Hyslop looked relieved.

"O. K. now," said Jimmie. "All teeth drawn."

"Will you turn the truck round, old son?" asked Hyslop anxiously. "We haven't a moment. Though I chose a lonely part, there's bound to be someone along soon... Ah, would you?" The prize-fighter had momentarily dropped his hands. "Turn your backs and face the hedge."

"Why not your car?" queried Rezaire as the pair, still surprised into silence by the swift turn of events, obediently turned.

"No, the truck. I'll explain later. Quick! I hear a car."

In a moment Jimmie had headed the van for London, and was moving slowly southward. Hyslop retreated backward for a dozen yards then turned and ran, leaping in at Jimmie's side.

"Clever boy!" chuckled Jimmie as they rushed back through the night air. "I hoped you'd spot that carpet dodge."

"Jolly nearly didn't. However, all's well that ends well."

"What about our two friends? They'll get your car out of the ditch and be after us."

"No fear!" Hyslop patted his pocket. "I've got a bit of its guts here. And anyway, they won't be after us for long. They've got a surprise coming!"

"What..." began Jimmie, when Hyslop interrupted with:

"Stop here, will you? I want to speak to this fellow."

They were entering a village and Jimmie drew up without question—for Hyslop seemed to have the business well in hand—but he nearly accelerated again as he saw by the roadside a policeman with a cycle.

This, however, was apparently what the young man wanted, for he leaned out and called to the constable in an assumed rough voice:

"Beg pardon, sir, but I think you ought to know, there's a couple of blokes some way back along the road that tried to stop us."

"Stop you! What for?" queried the policeman.

"Dunno. They'd got a big car and they were behaving queer. As though they'd pinched it and had a breakdown and wanted to get away. And when we didn't stop they tried to get onboard, and one of 'em hit me. Couple of rough lookin' ones, they was."

"Ho!" said the policeman sternly. "Did they?" He asked another question or two, and then got on his cycle and rode rapidly off towards what he evidently considered would be his promotion.

"Was that wise?" said Jimmie who had kept silent, concerned with concealing his shirt front.

"Absolute wisdom, old son. They can't get us now for stealing their truck, because we've accused them first."

"But..."

"Well, they don't know it yet, but that jolly old car is stolen. I took it from Greek Street tonight to follow up your bridal chariot."

Jimmie laughed so much that he nearly drove into the hedge.

* * * *

Throughout the long journey back towards London, Jimmie was explaining to his companion his knowledge of Number One's altered plans.

"Well," was Hyslop's comment when he finally had all the facts, "I think the whole thing's been jolly well worth it. But I say, old egg, haven't you been let in for a sticky time by this midnight rescue of mine?"

"When Number One hears of it,—yes."

"Then your safety rather depends on rounding up the troupe before they get a chance at you."

"It does," said Jimmie soberly.

"Looks as though we ought to call in a posse of police to help us," Hyslop suggested tactfully.

"I'm damned if I'll have 'busies' nosing about to help me," warmly replied his companion. "We can do it ourselves."

"How?"

"Well, I think Victoria Station at eleven A.M. on Wednesday will be our scene. As I told you, they've got to go by that train because I gather they've squared a Customs official at Calais who expects them by that boat, and they daren't run the risk of the French getting hold of it. Now, if we can fix a frame-up of our own at Victoria we ought to get them. I don't mind the police being drawn in afterwards to help us."

"Supposing they get past us?"

"Well," said Jimmie decisively, "I'm hanged if I don't go to Paris after them and get it there—before this Siminski."

"That's a risk, old lad."

"I know; but I'm going to pull off this job. Think of the money in it. I must remember, though, to get a passport from our 'Captain Smith.'"

"I've got one—all in order."

"Keep it! You may need it too."

"Gosh!" murmured Hyslop. "I *am* seeing life, what...? Well, here's London! What about abandoning this bus?"

* * * *

They left the truck in a side street in South Hampstead and a moment later picked up a taxi. Jimmie decided he might with safety pass the remainder of the night at the Grand Cross Hotel, though subsequently he would be wise to use his unknown hiding place in "The Vine." But he determined to sleep with door and window locked and a gun under his pillow. He was not going to underestimate Number One as an enemy.

As they parted, Hyslop reminded him that they were to be on hand at Viv's flat at ten o'clock; and Jimmie's heart suddenly sank. In the excitement of the last twelve hours he had forgotten this.

"I understand," continued Hyslop lightly, "that she's got some tough paying a visit and may want a little assistance."

"Yes," agreed Jimmie with a dry throat. All his old terror had returned. "Tough" did not describe Sam at all adequately. Everything seemed to be piling up on him at once. Sam was after him: Number One and his gang would soon be after him: yet, as he dropped wearily on to his bed, he smiled fitfully. He had his own brain and clever daring—a better weapon than the loud-voiced Sam's knife; and as for the spies, he had outwitted them once already, so surely he could do it again.

CHAPTER XII

SAM'S RETURN

Hyslop, waiting for Jimmie some way down Frith Street, picked him up at a discreet distance but did not join him till they sat casually side by side in the tube at Oxford Circus.

"And the business today?" asked Hyslop, when they had made sure they were not being observed.

"First, this damn fellow Sam," growled Jimmie. Sam now filled his thoughts to the exclusion of all else. Sam's unexpected return from America just at this junction threatened to upset all his plans.

"Oh, we'll settle him if he tries his naughty little tricks on Viv," answered Hyslop carelessly. "But what about the Number One Performin' Troupe?"

Jimmie tried to concentrate.

"I've been considering the matter," he said at last. "I see in the paper that our two friends of last night were safely pinched for stealing that car. I see too they've kept their mouths shut about us…"

"Good," put in Hyslop. "Then Number One won't know you've escaped?"

"Oh, he's bound to find out soon that I haven't been delivered at my destination. He may even, when he comes to hear how you rescued me, begin to suspect me of secret service, which will make things lively. The great point, however, is he certainly doesn't realize I know his intentions. And so," concluded Jimmie with a smile, "I'm going to rely absolutely on his not altering his plans again at this eleventh hour. If he does we're done."

"He may run a false scent just in case."

"He probably will; but *we* know he's tied to that particular train. And so our present scheme still stands… Now," he broke off, "today I want you to get in touch with Mario the little Italian waiter at the *Coin de Paradis*. To him I am the man who knows about Luigi and you can frighten him with that. I want you to make him promise that, if he learns anything which concerns me, he will phone instantly to…well, let's see, say to Viv's flat"

"Can we get him to promise? And will he keep it?"

"That depends on you," replied Jimmie. "You must put the fear of the Lord—and of me—into him. He'll have a good bit already, after last night. And here's a fiver to give him as well. Between the two he ought to promise."

Hyslop and Jimmie made a cautious entry into Viv's flat in Shrewsbury Mansions. They saw no spy of Sam's; indeed, Jimmie believed it would have been easy after all to have slipped in a couple of detectives and had Sam pulled. That would have got him out of the way for good. However, it was too late for that now, and anyway he was reluctant to have anything to do with the police.

They stayed chatting with Viv in her sitting-room for nearly an hour. Then the flat bell rang.

"Sam," whispered Viv, and the pair were hustled into hiding. They found themselves concealed by a thick curtain which hung across a corner behind a sofa. The one big window of the room was just on their left.

"Don't come out, Jimmie, unless I call you," pleaded Viv. "Honestly, Sam won't hurt me, but he might go for *you*, if he..."

"What about nice little me?" put in Hyslop humorously. "Don't nobody love me too!"

"And you, H.H.," added Viv, but something in her eyes told him he didn't count beside Jimmie—that strange man with so much ingenuity and so little physical courage.

Sam was shown in by Viv's maid, a dour female, who adored Viv and had no ideals whatsoever except loyalty to her mistress. Jimmie's heart leaped with a sudden terror as he once again heard his erstwhile partner's familiar overbearing tones, now tinged with an American accent. He had not heard that voice since their stand together in the Jermyn Street flat with the bullets smacking through the door. Sam's last words then as Jimmie, in panic-stricken desertion, whizzed to temporary safety down the outside lift, had been "You blasted little rat! I'll get you for this." And now he was in the same room.

"Well, Viv, ain't this just fine?" Sam was saying. "If you aren't a fine sight for a man, I don't know any."

Viv's eyebrows came together at the admiration in his tone. She had taken especial pains to dress in severe and unencouraging manner, but she could not help being a highly attractive girl.

"Well, Sam," she said coldly. "Sit down! What do you want? I can't spare much time."

"Nor can I," grinned Sam. "Do you know, Viv, my dear, I'm risking my life to come and see you. You won't give me away?"

"No."

"Ah, I knew you wouldn't."

"Not for any love of you," retorted Viv.

"Huh!" Sam was annoyed at this outspokenness. He realized at last that he was not going to make an easy conquest. "What's come over you? You ain't still sweet on that little…"

"What do you want?" she repeated, cutting him short.

"I've got a proposition, Viv," he said briskly. "I don't mind telling you, I'm doing well over here with some boys I know…"

"So I see in the papers."

"Oh! You guessed?" Sam didn't know whether to be pleased or annoyed. "Well, I gotta 'nother job or so and then I'm going back to Amurrica, the only country worth living in. To Chicago, too, the only town where a crook can earn a respectable living without being worried. Say, girlie, will you come with me? We'll work a…"

"No," said Viv.

"But I gotta scheme…"

"No." Viv rose and went to the bell.

"Viv, never mind the scheme. It's you I want. I'm just made for you. You an' me'll do fine together. Leave that dirty little rat Rezaire. See, I gotta car outside and I can take you somewhere safe right now."

"I'm quite safe here."

"You think so. Well, I tell you they're wise to you. You better come to safety with me. Someone's squealed."

"Liar!" remarked Viv dispassionately. "I know well no one's got anything on me."

Sam's bluff had failed. Jimmie, listening intently to the conversation, thought with scorn how Sam never had the intelligence to pull even the simplest bluff. And now of course he would try force; for at mention of the waiting car Jimmie realized Sam had come prepared to carry the girl off. And he knew what that would mean. There never was anything nice about Sam's methods.

He was right. Before Viv could reach the bell Sam had sprung. One arm pinioned hers; the other whipped a pad to her nose and mouth. Viv struggled, tried to call out, but only produced a frightened squeak.

Jimmie heard it and for a moment something conquered his fear so that he leaped out over the sofa into the room, knocking Hyslop back with his foot as he did so. He was almost on Sam when he saw the muzzle of Sam's revolver. Like a fool he had forgotten his own in that mad rush. He stopped short, fear claiming him again.

"Well, I'm—" ejaculated Sam. He let Viv, half unconscious, slip to the floor and restored the pad to his pocket. A sickly scent was in the air.

"You of all people, eh?" He kept the gun on Jimmie. "And yet I'm not surprised. S'pose this is your home now?"

Rezaire tried to speak; but found himself trembling at the thought that he had given himself over into Sam's hands. Then suddenly he realized that Hyslop was not with him. Late in getting out, the young man had grasped the situation and was now waiting a more favorable moment. Jimmie drew fresh hope.

"Come on, Sam," he said, as coolly as he could. "Put that gun up and let's talk. There's no sense in trying intimidation. You can't get what you want here!"

Sam grinned. He had grown a moustache and otherwise altered his appearance, but he looked as coarsely arrogant as ever.

"I've got more than I expected already. I didn't expect you and I owe you something," he added fiercely.

"And I owe you something. So let's call it quits and you clear out?"

Sam laughed derisively, and all at once Jimmie read his death in the cruel eyes, death for the enemy who was now a rival. He almost cowered as Sam replied:

"It'll take more than money or even a girl to make it quits between you and me, Rezaire! I got something here that's been waiting for you a long time." He slapped his thigh where Jimmie knew well lay the keen, evil-bladed knife which was Sam's favorite weapon.

Though his forehead was wet with his terror, Jimmie tried a last desperate throw.

"You fool," he said. "You won't get away from here. Don't you know Viv tipped you off? They're waiting outside."

"Liar!"

"You never did believe anything till you saw it, yet it's true."

"I wouldn't believe what you told me," laughed Sam, but under the laugh Jimmie now detected a little flavor of doubt. At once his fear began to vanish. A plan rapidly formed. He knew that the bone-headed Sam could always be worsted in an encounter of wits.

"Look for yourself!" he said. "There's one 'busy' in a grey hat directly opposite, watching your car, there are two at the back, and one in the hall below. You can see the chap opposite from this window, if you don't believe me."

Sam wavered. "Are you putting something across me?" he growled doubtfully. He took two steps to the window, then whirled round as if to catch Jimmie at some trick. But Rezaire had not moved a muscle.

"Go over to the far side of the room, face the wall and put your hands up," commanded Sam.

"What a lot of trouble to convince a big mutt!" sighed Jimmie, whose spirits had now risen. "Why don't you take my word?"

"Go on quick," countered Sam. Jimmie obeyed resignedly.

"Shall I turn when I've counted a hundred?" he asked. "Or will you call 'Coo-ee' when you've hidden?"

"You dare turn and I'll plug you," muttered Sam, then with four quick paces he had backed up to the window, his revolver still trained on Jimmie.

He turned his head over his shoulder to search the road, and as his eyes left his gun, a hand shot out from the curtain at his side and neatly plucked it from his grasp.

"No you don't, old love!" said Hyslop sweetly. Sam reaching for his knife, found himself studying the business end of his own revolver.

"All right, H.H.?" asked Jimmie, still face to the wall.

"All quiet on the Western front," said Hyslop coming out into the room. "Tut, tut!" he added as Sam let fly a string of obscenity on fully realizing how he had been tricked.

Jimmie ran to Viv, who though now conscious again, was still lying where she had been dropped, looking very white.

"How are you feeling, Viv?" asked Rezaire anxiously, lifting her to a chair. She seemed very soft and fragile, quite unlike the clever self-reliant girl he knew so well.

"I shall be all right in a minute. Jimmie, you are a dear," she whispered. She made as if to put her arms impulsively round his neck as he bent over her, then changed her mind. "Thank you so much," she concluded quietly.

"Nothing at all," muttered Jimmie.

"Never mind. I love you for it," she added lightly, looking up at him.

Jimmie stammered a moment and then asked abruptly: "What are we to do with Sam?"

At mention of his name Sam cursed Jimmie again, till Hyslop grimly forced him into a corner.

"Naughty! Naughty!" he said reproachfully. "If you use words like that, my little man, you'll…"

"Oh, go to hell!"

"Well, if you haven't finished my sentence perfectly!" retorted Hyslop admiringly.

* * * *

At the end of ten minutes' whispered conversation Sam's future had been decided upon. Jimmie, whose fear of his enemy was only increased by the knowledge that he had worsted him once more, had even, against his earlier inclination, desired to hand him over to the police, but both Viv and Hyslop argued very strongly against it. They both pointed out, speaking in whispers, that at this critical juncture of their own affair, they could not run the risk of being involved with Scotland Yard.

"You see, *you're* all right, Jimmie," said Viv, "but up to recently H.H. and I were working the shops, and I think Sam may have a line on us. At any rate it'd probably mean our being watched, just when we want to be free."

Jimmie had at last reluctantly agreed to letting Sam go, under promise that he let them alone and went straight back to the States. If he stayed In London or if he tried to interfere again, they would tip him off to the police.

"And you know what that means," said Jimmie to him significantly, as Sam stood at the door glowering. "The nine o'clock walk for you with a nice bit of hemp at the end of it."

Sam only growled.

"And it's no good trying to get back on me, because I've done my stretch and I'm running straight. Now, get!"

"Good-bye, baby," added Hyslop sweetly.

As he went Sam turned and snarled: "By God, Rezaire, I'll get you for this some time."

"Not in this country," bluffed Jimmie swiftly. "In case of an accident I'm leaving a note for the police to say you did it."

From the window all three watched Sam sullenly cross the road to a waiting car.

"I wish to the devil," muttered Jimmie fretfully, "we'd done something else."

"He'll go back all right," said Viv reassuringly. "I know Sam."

"Yes. But he may have a last shot at me first. Thank God he doesn't know where I hang out."

* * * *

After talking their future plans over with Viv, Jimmie and Hyslop left very discreetly, Jimmie carefully turning on his tracks several times in case he had been picked up on leaving Shrewsbury Mansions by any friend of Sam's.

Arriving at last in a public call box in Piccadilly, he phoned to Gullidge. He wanted to get in touch with 'Captain Smith' about a passport, so that, in the event of failure at Victoria on the morrow, he could go over to Paris for one last attempt.

Inspector Gullidge was frankly offensive about the previous night's effort, when a body of police had been kept standing by at a police station, only to receive Viv's message that they were not wanted.

"And how many constables will you want today, *Mister* Rezaire?" was the gist of his sarcasm, and it made Jimmie more than ever determined to lay the spies by the heels without any official assistance.

From 'Captain Smith' he extracted a reluctant promise that a passport for France would be ready for him at Scotland Yard that afternoon. 'Captain Smith' was skeptical about France, doubtful now about the wisdom of ever having let Rezaire into the game. He again intimated that he had his own ideas on how and where the Murchison sighter was going to leave England, and this time Jimmie was careful not to mention the East Coast or to say anything to shake his confidence.

After telephoning, he embarked, with Hyslop's help, upon some preparatory arrangements. He paid his bill at the Grand Cross and got his effects taken away secretly from the hotel which now he no longer considered safe. Some he dispatched circuitously to "The Vine," others to Viv's flat. He also had a specially packed suitcase deposited ready in Victoria Station cloak room; for some intuition told him that he might need to go to Paris in a hurry before he had seen this matter through.

Hyslop then went off to get in touch with Mario as prearranged, and after that to go to Shrewsbury Mansions and lie low. Though Jimmie intended to sleep that night in the obscurity of "The Vine" in order to be safe from Sam, Viv's flat was to be their headquarters for the next few hours up to what he hoped would be their final coup at Victoria Station. In the middle of the crowd there, Jimmie felt no doubt that he and Hyslop, posing as detectives, would be able to hold up the innocent-looking spies, who, up till that moment, would be secure in the assumption that no one could possibly know their plans.

After parting from his companion, Jimmie went down to an obscure restaurant in West Kensington to get his lunch. On the way back he changed his bus twice almost as soon as he had boarded it, and in other ways covered his tracks. He was feeling decidedly jumpy; for by now it was certain that Number One knew that he had not arrived safely at the "Gables," in which case it was highly probable that suspicion had been really roused at last.

To his relief he saw no one in the least doubtful, and so came at last to Whitehall where he received his passport from an uncommunicative and suspicious looking official. He then walked down Whitehall and along to Piccadilly Circus. Deep in thought he found he had passed Shaftesbury Avenue. When, turning to retrace his steps, he gave a start of surprise. Coming towards him was no less a person than Monsieur Villon, the stout proprietor of the *Coin de Paradis* restaurant.

CHAPTER XIII

A MARKED MAN

At first Jimmie wondered if he had been followed; then realized that Monsieur Villon, who was just out for an afternoon's stroll near his restaurant, was not the type to follow people about. For a moment he hesitated, wondering whether he should turn hastily and seek to avoid recognition; then he braced himself up as he realized that the encounter was, after all, not so terrible. At the most, the fat man would tell the spies that night that he had met Jimmie; but they of course would already know that he was not where they had tried to put him. On the other hand, the meeting might even be helpful, for by a few skillful words, he might perhaps convey to his enemies an impression of innocence in spite of last night's happenings.

So when the little man would have waddled past, he stopped him with a greeting.

Monsieur Villon peered at him through his thick pince-nez, moving his bushy grey eyebrows interrogatively.

"Aha!" he puffed at last, beaming largely. "One of my clients, is it not? One meets them everywhere, yes? But with such a restaurant, *que voulez vous*?"

"Exactly," smiled Jimmie. "Well, how are you? I didn't see you last night. You weren't ill, I hope?"

"Ah no, monsieur, I go to see my brother, because it was his fete day. He is manager of the Rizzi Grill Room. He…"

"Indeed." Jimmie cut him short. "Well, I'm sorry you were absent, or you might have been of assistance to me. I'm afraid I had a drop too much last night in that upper room, and Mr. Neasden played a joke on me." Monsieur Villon made a deprecating "Chk! Chk!" with his mouth. "He had me put in a truck that was going out of London, so I gather. I must have fallen out after a while, because I was picked up this morning by a milk cart."

"Too bad, monsieur, too bad!"

"Do you know why he did it?" asked Jimmie shrewdly. "I don't want to offend him. I am particularly anxious to keep in with him," he added with a hint of mystery.

M. Villon was at a complete loss for a motive. He was obviously on Jimmie's side in the matter, though he would not say anything outright, and they parted amicably after a minute's conversation.

Jimmie walked on towards Trafalgar Square.

He was not very hopeful of the spies being deceived by Villon's account of how he had taken the matter of the doped coffee; but he had thought it worth trying. For there was yet a chance, since the two men were still in prison, that Number One had not heard the full story of his escape from the truck and the fact that an accomplice had helped him. In which case Villon's report might just serve to keep the spies doubtful for a little longer of how to treat him, and might prevent Number One guessing at Jimmie's connection with the Secret Service. For when he did, there would be danger of the worst kind ahead.

* * * *

Rezaire spent the afternoon in a secluded corner of the lounge of the Piccadilly Hotel, where he felt he was safe from observation. He wanted to think out his plans, to foresee and prepare for all possible contingencies. Though he still felt positive that the stolen sighter was going away by that eleven o'clock train tomorrow, particularly since Number One had now skillfully got the Secret Service working on a false Yarmouth trail, yet some last minute hitch might occur. However, he was prepared. Both he and Hyslop had passports and were ready to go to France at a moment's notice and even bring the thing back by force—though Jimmie would have preferred to round up the whole gang as well if it were possible.

He rose at last and sauntered out. At Piccadilly Circus he phoned to Viv to find out if Hyslop had reported the result of his interview with Mario, but was told he had not yet turned up.

Emerging again from the booth he paused at the corner of the Haymarket. While deliberating where to go next, he felt suddenly and unaccountably nervous, as though he were being watched. His mind flashed fearfully to Sam and his threats. He had been a fool to let Sam go. He…

At that moment a scrap of paper was deftly thrust into his hand. Wheeling round quickly he recognized vanishing in the crowd the same seedy little man who had first spoken to him five days ago when, just out of prison, he sat in St. James' Park. And on that occasion the man had been the messenger of Number One's gang. A new and terrible fear drove all thought of Sam from his mind.

With trembling fingers he unfolded the paper. In type he read: "We have a way with traitors. Say good-bye. No. 1."

Jimmie looked round in wild terror. He was being followed after all. Rashly he had relied too much on allaying Number One's suspicions through Monsieur Villon, forgetting that Number One was no fool himself, and would have seen through the bluff. And now—he licked his dry lips—now the spies had marked him down as a dangerous traitor—too dangerous to live.

With an abrupt motion he turned and almost ran into the tube station behind him, hurried into a lift which was half full and watched narrowly all those who entered after him. There were about a dozen of them and Jimmie memorized the features of each one. At the bottom he entered a train, got out at the next station, and dodging hurriedly through the passages jumped into a train returning in the opposite direction, thus doubling on his tracks. Back at Piccadilly, he entered the lift and once more scrutinized everyone who followed him in.

He recognized no one. With a sigh of relief, he emerged once again into the comforting roar of Piccadilly Circus. The crowd stilled the panic in his heart. Thence he made his way on foot to a place where he intended to have an early dinner; for he knew he had a busy day on the morrow; and it was already dusk.

Half-way there he saw a public telephone box at a corner of a quiet street, and remembered he must ring Viv again for news of Hyslop. As he made for it, an old gentleman, descending from a taxi, did the same. Though Jimmie was first, he stood aside; not from politeness, but because he did not want anyone listening outside while he phoned.

The old man passed inside, without acknowledging the courtesy, failed apparently to find his pennies and in another moment came out again grumbling to himself. He held the door open for Jimmie who thanked him and passed in. As the door shut Jimmie heard a faint crackle of glass. It did not arouse his curiosity, but a second later his nostrils were caught by a queer pungent odor.

Jimmie recognized it in a flash. It was cyanic acid gas; it spelled death, rapid and certain…

He gripped instantly at the door-handle; but could not move it. It was held fast by the old man outside, who, after dropping the deadly little glass vial for Jimmie's feet to crush, had neatly ushered him into what was now nothing less than a swift lethal chamber.

Jimmie's brain was trained to work like lightning in an emergency. He did not bother to wrestle with the handle against someone apparently as strong as himself for the few short moments before the fumes overcame him. There could be only one end to that. Instead, like a flash, he doubled his feet up against the opposite wall and with his back against the door put all his love of life into one stupendous heave of his whole body.

The leverage gained was terrific; he had the full power of back and stomach muscles. The door burst open, knocking his enemy backward. Taking gulps of sweet fresh air, Jimmie found himself sprawling on the pavement.

From the agility with which the old man gained his feet, Jimmie realized now it was a young man disguised. Before he himself was properly up, the taxi, still prowling in support for the purpose, had snapped up his opponent and was off in a flash. Pursuit on foot was hopeless. He was beaten; though he was lucky to be alive.

As he opened his mouth to swear, an excited voice behind him cried: "Hop in, quick! I'll catch him."

The sheerest luck had helped Jimmie at that instant. Of the few spectators of the strange incident, one was a young man in a powerful car. Next moment his assailant was being rapidly overhauled.

Though the taxi twisted and turned in and out of side-streets, it now had no chance of escape; and its occupant soon realized this. Jimmie, eyes glued on the vehicle ahead, suddenly saw a figure, now no longer wearing a white beard, leap from the door and disappear like a rabbit up a narrow passage for pedestrians only.

With a sweep and a hum of powerful brakes, the sporting unknown brought his car also opposite the passage.

"Jump and run!" he cried, and with a shouted "Thank you" Jimmie did so, blessing his helper's keenness and presence of mind. Ahead of him ran his quarry and Jimmie felt for the gun in his side pocket. Passers-by stared open mouthed, but made no attempt to interfere.

The flying figure reached the end of the passage and, as it turned into the street, collided with a passing policeman who instantly barred the way. The next moment Jimmie had come up in triumph.

"Now then," began the constable, "what's up?"

But Jimmie, about to speak, only stared in surprise at his opponent. For this man who had just tried to murder him was none other than the little clean-shaven man with the gap in his teeth, whom he had seen lunching with Zita in the *Coin de Paradis* a few days ago and had never seen since—one of the spies of Number One's gang.

Before he could recover from his amazement, the other had stepped forward, determined, now he could not escape by flight, to bluff his way out.

"That man, constable," he accused coolly, in the same queer voice which sounded as though it were disguised, "is a bad character. He threatened me with violence and then pursued me."

Jimmie rapidly considered his position. He foresaw his opponent's game—a false accusation, righteous anger, a magnanimous refusal at the end to make a charge, and a request to the constable to detain the assailant, till the poor victim was out of sight. He countered at once:

"He's lying, constable. It's the other way about. I accuse *him* of snatching a wad of notes out of my hand a minute ago. That's why I was chasing him."

"What a preposterous story!" flamed the other, taken aback by Jimmie's swift and equally false retort.

"You know it's true…"

"'Ere, 'ere," put in the policeman scratching his head. "Stop it! You better both come along with me to the Station, and 'ave it out there." This was exactly what Jimmie had played for; and he agreed eagerly. The spy protested at first, but the constable was firm.

"Both of you's made a direc' charge," he said, "and it's got to be gorn into. The other gent's willing, sir, so it'll look funny to me if you ain't." At this the spy gave in, realizing that he was only bringing suspicion on himself. They moved off to the police station, the center of a small crowd. Jimmie was racking his brains all the time, trying to put his finger on a vague elusive memory, latent in the other's voice.

* * * *

Before a slow and massive Station Sergeant the two faced one another, the constable in close attendance. The little man, confidently master of himself once more, was displaying a well-bred annoyance, but Jimmie sensed somehow a nervousness underneath, and did some rapid thinking. He had got his man to the police-station all right; the thing was to keep him there. How could it be done? The false accusation had played its part and could be taken no further. Yet he could do little good by bringing up the telephone-booth incident. No Station Sergeant would believe a wild story about poison gas and people disguised in white beards, fabricated apparently after arrival at the police-station; and he could see that the man with the gap in his teeth, scowling at him opposite, knew this well. For him to take that line, truth though it was, would be a false move; and in a few minutes the spy would be free to walk out, leaving Jimmie embroiled with the police and threatened with an imaginary libel action. If only he could place that voice with the disguised tones…

"What is the meaning of this absurd charge?" The other was already beginning his attack. "Here is my card! You will see I am an army captain.

May I ask who this"—he surveyed Jimmie up and down—"this—er—stranger is?"

The Station Sergeant was writing busily.

"'Arf a minute, Captain, please... Now do you make a charge? You say this gennelman threatened you with valence?"

"He brings a charge of robbery against me, I think. Let him substantiate it if he can. And quickly; I'm on my way to keep an important engagement!"

Luckily the Station Sergeant was not a man to be hurried.

"All in good time, sir. You gennelmen can't go starting this sort of thing and then runnin' away. This 'as to be thrashed out thorough and right now."

"But look here, Sergeant, it's a matter of life and death. I'm a doctor."

Though slow, the Station Sergeant was sure.

"Then why does your visiting card say *Captain*?" he asked after a pause.

Jimmie admired the way in which the spy without a second's hesitation replied:

"My dear fellow, have you never heard of an Army Doctor?"

"With private patients?" swiftly interpolated Rezaire.

"Did I say so?..."

"Now, now." The sergeant was worried. "Anyway, sir, even if you're a doctor you'll have to stay for a minute and explain."

Jimmie, watching his man intently, saw a flicker of fear pass across the other's face. Momentarily he put his hand to his mouth with a quick, nervous action.

At this point a blinding light suddenly broke on Rezaire. What a fool he had been!..."

"Now, sir"—the Station Sergeant had turned back to him—"what is this charge you bring? Robbery?"

Jimmie looked his opponent straight in the eyes. He had him now. For the quick nervous action had been, in spite of the fact that he was clean-shaven, a movement to pull a moustache, and it had set off his memory along the correct channels at last. No wonder the disguised voice had a familiar ring.

"I accuse this man of murder," he said quietly.

The constable dropped a glove. The sergeant opened his mouth. The little man's face was pale, the gap in his teeth showing black in his amazement and fear.

"Wha—what d'you mean?" he gasped, and then pulled himself together to add haughtily: "Is this a joke?"

Jimmie gave a short exultant laugh. In those first few words, surprised out of him, the other had for once forgotten to disguise his voice. And, as he had but the moment before realized, it was the voice he had heard that Friday night across the body of the dead Secret Service man. This man with the gapped teeth was one and the same person as the murderer, Davis,—whose face Jimmie had not seen in full light at the time,—Davis, his moustache shaved off and a disguised voice in Jimmie's presence.

The Station Sergeant had recovered.

"Are you mad?" he said with some reason.

"I—I don't understand this outrage," stormed Davis, also recovering his nerve, as he realized what slender ground his accuser must stand upon. But despite his acting, Jimmie perceived how nervous he was, for he kept rubbing his sweating palms furtively against his trousers. This last suddenly gave his clever brain a fresh idea.

"I'm not mad," he said coolly and produced a note-book from his pocket. From this he tore a leaf. "I accuse this man, known I believe as Davis, of the murder in Warsaw Street on the evening of Friday, October 12th. This will show you where I got my proof," he added to Davis, and handed him the small sheet of paper.

Curious to know what he had to refute, Davis extended his hand and took it. Then:

"What fooling is this?" he snapped, hope again replacing the fear in his eyes. For the paper was bare, a blank sheet.

Jimmie took it back very, very carefully, picked up an envelope from the desk and put the paper inside.

"You can't keep me here," said Davis angrily, "on these ridiculous charges! Why, I happen to know," he added turning to the sergeant and playing his trump card, "that this man is an ex-convict."

"'Ere, 'ere!" began the sergeant taking charge once more. Jimmie's strange and deliberate actions had held him spellbound as if by a conjuring trick. "Now you say…"

"One minute!" interrupted Jimmie authoritatively. "Sergeant, I call upon you to detain this man…"

"You can't keep me…"

"…Until Inspector Gullidge of Scotland Yard has seen the fingerprints on the paper inside that envelope, which you should send to him at once. They will be quite clear because his hand was greasy, and on the forefinger of the right hand there will in all probability be a scar in the shape of a cross. Inspector Gullidge will like to compare them with those on the handle of the stiletto, with which the Warsaw Street murder was committed…"

Any further doubt in the mind of the sergeant was dispelled by the sudden dash which Davis made for the door at this unexpected piling up of facts. A constable just outside caught him neatly—but only Jimmie had noticed that Davis had made his rush apparently in response to a quick double hoot from a motor-car outside. It told him that Number One was indeed not an opponent to be underestimated.

* * * *

Jimmie mopped his forehead as he came out of the police-station half an hour later. One of the gang at least was now under lock and key. Even Gullidge had grudgingly congratulated him, arriving hot-foot, after he had compared the records of the stiletto handle finger-prints with those that sprang to light under treatment on the blank page of Jimmie's note-book. 'Captain Smith' had also been sent for to examine the prisoner, but Jimmie realized that Davis probably had great faith in Number One's ability to help him, even now, and so would not give away any information—except perhaps a deliberate clue about Yarmouth. Rezaire concluded, therefore, that Number One would not change his plans for tomorrow on account of this mishap.

He stood on the edge of the curb and pondered. His knowledge of the gang was clearer, now that he realized that Davis the murderer and the smooth-shaven man he had seen lunching with Zita were the same person. It removed, so to speak, two of his opponents at one blow. He had now against him Number One himself—mysterious and as yet completely unknown, a highly dangerous enemy; then the big-nosed, loose-limbed Neasden,—cruel and efficient under his mask of pedantic politeness; and Zita—a cunning little devil, probably their decoy, but thank Heaven Jimmie was not the man to be laid low by her accustomed weapon of sex. In addition, there were several minor characters and subordinates; for instance, Monsieur Villon, not dangerous, but evidently bound to Number One's chariot; Mario, who might now be reckoned as a friend and ally; the little seedy messenger,—harmless; and others unknown, such as the taxi man who had supported Davis after his attempt in the telephone booth. There was, too, the ferrety-faced watcher—no, he was Sam's…

Heavens! Jimmie's heart sank, as he realized what he had momentarily forgotten—that Sam was against him as well…

At that moment some instinct, working apart from his busy brain, made him step quickly back from the curb. Three seconds after a powerful car went past at a high speed. Jimmie had barely realized that, if he had not stepped back, the car in all probability would have purposely mounted the pavement, knocked him down, and disappeared before anyone discovered it was not a genuine accident, when he heard a low "Phtt" instantly followed by a sharp smack on the wall by his head.

In a blind panic he darted back into the safety of the police-station. A constable laughed at him, but then he had not heard, as Jimmie had, the discharge of a revolver fitted with a silencer, or the impact of the bullet at his ear.

Number One worked swiftly; and Jimmie was now a marked man.

CHAPTER XIV

IN VIV'S FLAT

Rezaire spent ten minutes in the safety of the station, recovering from the effect of this fresh attempt on his life. Then he borrowed the police phone to call Viv's flat. He had begun to feel afraid that his ubiquitous enemy had discovered his connection with Viv and Hyslop and had made use of it. To his relief Viv was quite safe and unworried, and Hyslop himself spoke a moment later.

From him he learned that Mario had been interviewed with satisfactory results, though first he had had to be assured that he was not being held to blame for Jimmie's having taken the drugged coffee despite his warning. Mario, it transpired further, was very angry with Neasden over some insult and had hardly needed to be threatened with Jimmie's weapon of betrayal to Luigi. His gratitude for the five pounds had been overwhelming and once he had realized that Jimmie was now actually working against Neasden, he had volunteered to let him know anything he could find out, though that day, he asserted, the place had been empty of the gang and he had learned nothing.

This news cheered Rezaire, and he felt that if he came through the night safely he might very well have the game in his hands. Nevertheless he left the police-station by the back way, dodging and twisting to throw watchers off his track. He ate a solitary meal in a quiet restaurant in Edgware Road, sitting with his back to a wall and facing the only entrance.

After dinner Rezaire visited Viv. Hyslop had gone and Jimmie found the girl suffering from a bad attack of nerves. She had taken off her dress and was in a dressing gown in front of the fire. Jimmie felt a quick catch of the heart when he saw her. He remembered how well he had known her in the old days; and looked into her piquant little face with a new emotion when he realized that her nerves and her fear this night were on his behalf.

After he had made light of his escapes that afternoon, they talked for a long time in half-whispers, recalling old adventures shared before Jimmie "went into the country." But all Viv's terror seemed to come back, when at last Jimmie stood up to go. Her face became white and her eyes widened with fear.

"Jimmie boy, are you sure it's safe?"

"Yes," said Jimmie assuming a confidence he was not feeling. "I know I've slipped the Number One lot for the time. And I didn't see Sam or his little ferret as I came in. I expect he's thought better of it and cleared out."

"Shall I ring up H.H. and get him to come round and go back with you? He's at a hotel near here tonight so as to be on the phone. I don't think they're wise to him yet."

"No, no, Viv. I'm all right."

"Jimmie!" The girl stood up suddenly facing him by the fireside. "Jimmie, you're safe here, aren't you?"

"Yes."

"Well—why not stay here?" She stood facing him, her alluring foreign-looking face tilted up towards his. To Jimmie suddenly she looked the most wonderful thing in the world. All his old passion for her rushed back on him, and in that moment he knew there never had been anybody but Viv.

"You did love me once, Jimmie," she said softly.

"But," stammered Jimmie, "I—I can't stay. Think of our job tomorrow. Think of..."

To his surprise Viv burst into tears. She had been living under a great strain, physical, mental and emotional for the last week, and now it suddenly came to a climax. But chief of all was the emotional strain, for she had discovered in the last days that she wanted Jimmie after all—always had wanted Jimmie. She had undertaken this work with him simply to help him and to be near him. She knew his weaknesses, his vanity and his cowardice, and yet she desired him for her own.

"What—what's up?" cried Jimmie seizing her arms.

In a moment Viv had gained control over herself.

"Are you blind, Jimmie?" she whispered. "Don't you know what everyone seems to know; H.H. and even Sam?"

"Oh." Jimmie had known, but somehow had not allowed himself to admit it. He hardened himself. "Viv, honestly, don't let's talk about anything tonight."

"All right," replied Viv dully, and turned away to stare into the fire.

Jimmie, after peeping cautiously round the side of the window curtain, went to the door.

Then he stopped abruptly, came back, and seizing Viv, kissed her with passion and hunger.

"Oh!" cried the girl in a new voice, as he dropped her and went to the door once more. "Then—then you *do*?"

"Of course I do, you little fool!" said the man, his fingers on the handle. "Perhaps the blind have been leading the blind!"

Then he went.

Jimmie walked rapidly down Edgware Road. He was apparently unconscious of a taxi that had emerged from a side road and was now crawling up behind, as if looking for fares.

But Jimmie was rarely unconscious of what went on round him; particularly since he knew, as he did now, that Number One had him marked. A queer sense of humor took charge of him, an expression of happiness that pervaded him after feeling Viv's lips under his. He paused by a lamp and wrote something on a sheet of his notebook, folded it up, addressed it and had moved on, before the taxi caught up with him.

Further on he stopped once more, this time conveniently near a policeman. He was not running the risk of being attacked openly.

"Taxi, sir?" queried the driver at last coming up level.

"Are you engaged?" asked Rezaire with caution.

"No, sir."

"Then I'll engage you."

"Right, sir." The flag tinkled down. "Where to?"

"Do you know the *Coin de Paradis* restaurant in Warsaw Street?"

The man as nearly as possible started, but said: "I'll find it, sir."

"Good! Well, I'm not going myself," smiled Jimmie, handing him the little note, "but I want you to take this note there, and ask for a gentleman called Number One. Here's five bob, and..."

But with a snarl of rage, the man cast an apprehensive glance at the policeman, snatched at the note and drove rapidly off without even bothering about the money.

Jimmie, smiling thoughtfully, vanished down a side-street. He felt pleased with himself at the incident and nearly laughed out loud. For inside the note was pencilled: "Love and kisses to No. 1 from his own little Jimmie."

* * * *

Rezaire arrived some while later by cautious methods at "The Vine" private door, let himself in and went silently upstairs. He entered his room with a sigh of relief. Before switching on the light,—for he knew all the tricks,—he locked the door, crossed the room to the window which he always kept fastened while out, opened it to air the room for a while and pulled down the blind. Then at last he snapped up the switch—and his mouth fell open with a wild exclamation of terror.

Sitting on the bed, knife in hand and an evil grin on his face, was Sam.

CHAPTER XV

TWO'S COMPANY

Jimmie Rezaire dropped his hand at once to his hip pocket, but Sam snapped in a fierce whisper:

"I can chuck this through your throat before you can get it out."

Jimmie faltered, frozen with terror. Sam, lounging over with his long, evil knife ready, took Jimmie's gun from his pocket and threw it contemptuously on the bed.

"Two's company, eh?" he observed as he sat down again. "Say, you didn't think we'd meet again, didja? You thought I'd go back to the States like a good little boy? I suppose you thought, too, that I didn't know of your bolt-hole here? Well, I'm as good a trailer as you are, see?"

Jimmie did not bother to ask how he had found out. The thing was he had done so—and he saw murder in Sam's eyes. He tried to collect his wits to deal with the situation, but a wild fright had scattered them headlong.

Sam was talking. He talked through his teeth, and under his words there ran a current of burning revenge which had found its victim, and primitive cruelty which at last had an object. He talked, while his enemy stood silent, his fascinated eyes always on the shining knife, of how Jimmie had betrayed him and left him to the police. He talked of all he had done for Jimmie, conveniently forgetting the scores of times that Jimmie's quick brain had saved him. He talked with pent-up hatred of that morning's encounter, when Jimmie had come between him and his desire.

"By God," he said still in the low, threatening tones, "by the time I've finished with you, Viv won't be able to think of you except as a hospital exhibit... Stand still, or I'll begin now!" he threatened as Jimmie stirred slightly at mention of the girl's name... "I'm going to cut you up like a nigger once showed me, and after that you won't bother me. Then I'll have Viv. I'll teach her to call me over like she did. Do you know what I'm going to do to that piece? I'm going to..."

"Shut up!" said Jimmie sharply. The mention of Viv, from whom he had just come, seemed to give him courage. To his surprise Sam did shut up, momentarily disconcerted.

Jimmie had an idea. Sam was banking too much on his fear of moving and on his own skill with the knife. If he could snap the light out, he might just get the gun from the bed before Sam got it, and before Sam's knife got him. A slender chance. And if he succeeded it would probably mean murder; but anything was better than torture at the hands of Sam.

He went suddenly cold as Sam got up at that moment and walked over to him, balancing his blade between his fingers. He tried to leap for the light-switch, but not a muscle moved to his will. He was again chained by terror.

With the air of an inquisitive doctor, Sam pressed the point of the knife against the other's chest, till Jimmie shrank suddenly as the steel penetrated the cloth and just pierced the skin. He did this two or three times in varying parts of the body, laughing evilly as Jimmie quivered from the terror of the touch rather than from actual pain.

"Just reconnoitering," volunteered Sam pleasantly. "Going to have a real dig soon, but first I'm going to stop your mouth."

He moved over to the washstand by the window to get a towel, but he faced Jimmie all the time.

At the window he paused reflectively. "Or how'd it be," he whispered, as if the idea had just struck him, "if I cut your little tongue out? Save me trouble, and I've often wondered what sort of noise a man would make."

Jimmie nearly felt sick. He must do something—must make a fight for life. His knees were shaking, he felt sure his terror would not allow him to move; yet he tried to calculate the distance from his left hand to the switch. And at any rate Sam was now by the window, further almost than he was from the revolver on the bed.

As he saw quick decision come into Sam's eyes, he made a superhuman effort; and jumped. A whistling gasp of pent-up fear left his chest, though he did not know he had made it, as his trembling fingers leaped towards the switch.

He saw Sam's knife hand jerk back to throw, in a terrible silence— then several things happened at once...

First, distinct in the stillness, there sounded a muffled "Phtt" ; then Sam's arm suddenly paused in its swift upward movement as if caught by an invisible hand; and his forehead seemed all in a moment to turn ghastly red, as though a great patch of skin had been peeled from it. In the same instant Jimmie's fingers closed on the switch and darkness flickered down on the scene, followed by a sudden snap as the spring blind unaccountably jerked up to the roller...

Next minute Jimmie found himself, with his stomach thudding up and down, lying on the bed with his hand round the blessed revolver, and the lingering vision of Sam's scarlet forehead mirrored against the darkness of the room.

But the room itself was as silent as death...

* * * *

Lying there Rezaire almost fainted with the horror of what he had gone through, and the inexplicable happenings of the last few seconds; but the knowledge that Sam, though suddenly and unaccountably silent, was still somewhere in the room, kept him tense and ready for anything.

After a moment he gathered courage to move slightly. He sat up on the bed and, with the revolver at guard, whispered hysterically: "Sam, if you stir I'll shoot."

There was no answer, still no movement. In the faint light which came from outside now the blind had mysteriously flicked up; Jimmie, peering forward, at last made out a dark mass. He bent out and touched it; even shook it. It was limp and warm. Sam was dead.

Rezaire, calmer now, began to puzzle over what had happened. He knew he had not touched Sam. What then had killed him, causing his forehead to go red in that ghastly manner? Why too had the spring blind flicked up? He recalled suddenly the noise he had heard as Sam jerked his hand back to throw; and that gave him the clue. It was the same noise he had heard that afternoon when the attempt was made on his life as he stood outside the police station—the report of a silenced revolver. Sam had been shot through the back of the head, the flattened bullet coming out, redly horrible, at his forehead. It followed, therefore, that Sam had been shot from outside through the open window; and it was the passage of the bullet through the drawn blind which had caused it to spring up so suddenly. But who had shot Sam? And why?

Jimmie sat and considered. Then creeping to the window, he peered cautiously over the ledge, and there the explanation came to him. It was not Sam, but he, who should have received that bullet. From the roof parapet on the left to his window was an easy range for a man who could see his target outlined for him by the electric light on the blind; and from the parapet to the *Coin de Paradis* attic was only a short journey. It was Number One again. Number One then who must know of this room. Bitterly he perceived that the hiding place he thought so secure had been known to both his enemies.

He pondered deeply. At any rate he was now safe for a while from Number One's attentions. The unknown who had fired the shot had no reason to believe he had killed any other than the man he intended. He would not even have known there were two people in the room; for Sam had spoken in whispers before the shot, and there had been silence after, and even the switching off of the light, which might have betrayed the presence of another person, had occurred so immediately that the murderer might very well suppose his bullet, after finding its mark, to have passed on and broken the electric globe. And the room had been hidden in darkness by the time the blind snapped up to reveal it.

Slowly Jimmie's spirits revived and then a sudden unreasoning panic gripped him again, as he reflected that the spies might yet enter the room from the roof to make certain. Seizing his revolver, he fled out leaving the bedroom as it was, but locking the door. Outside he felt better. At least he could thank Number One for one thing: by killing the half-mad Sam he had saved the very life he was trying to destroy.

Recklessly, his fear still on him, Jimmie took the first taxi that offered and drove northward.

* * * *

Viv's maid, knowing Jimmie, let him in at the flat door, vanishing as her mistress appeared from the bedroom. Viv still wore the dressing gown, but underneath she now had thin silk pajamas and her dark hair was tumbled about her piquant face.

"Jimmie, what is it?" she cried.

"I—I've come back," he said, "after—after all."

His terror was obvious in his every action, but Viv only smiled a triumphant and happy smile. For Jimmie Rezaire's fear was her best friend. Once it had saved her from prison; now it had given her the man she loved.

CHAPTER XVI

A CHANGE OF PLAN

It was nine o'clock. Hyslop had come round after an early breakfast and he and Jimmie were now making final preparations for their expected capture at Victoria in about an hour and a half's time.

With the morning, Jimmie had recovered his spirits, and whistled gaily as he moved about the flat. Sam's death had lifted from his mind the load of fear which had lain there all the years, ever since, exasperated at Sam's selfish stupidity, he had first left him to his fate; added to which he had at last found the love and comfort which only Viv could really give him. Finally, he now felt certain of a successful ending to his self-undertaken venture. For Number One, secure under the impression he had removed his main opponent at last, would fall ripely into his hands at Victoria, Jimmie was overwhelmingly curious to meet this unknown opponent with whom he had crossed swords so often during the last few days.

In the lightness of heart which had come to him, Jimmie had perhaps slightly underestimated Number One's intelligence; for at that moment the telephone bell rang. Viv went to it.

"Hullo!" she answered. "Yes. Detective Inspector who...? Well, what is it?" Jimmie stiffened to attention and stole to her side to listen. He wondered what on earth the police could want with Viv. Hyslop also approached silently.

"Yes, I know him," Viv was saying casually, though her face had become suddenly pale. To Jimmie she indicated with a little nod that he was the subject of inquiry, but Jimmie by then had his ear to the extra receiver. He heard an official voice, whose he did not know:

"...course you know he's only just out of prison?"

"Oh, yes," said Viv, in control of herself once more. She was far too clever at once to deny stupidly all knowledge of the person that the police were after. There were better methods. Jimmie himself had taught her the value of a well-prepared bed of truth to take the planted lie.

"Seen him lately?" continued the man imperturbably.

"Yes. Quite a lot. He's a friend of mine, you know. He's running straight now. Got into some business which he…"

"*When* did I see him last?" The soil was now ready for Viv's lie. "Why, only last night. Yes, about nine, or half past, I suppose. Then he went away. I don't know where he's living, but I think it's a hotel in Trafalgar Square. Anyway, I'm expecting him here today, after lunch." Every word bore the imprint of absolute truth.

"I don't think you'll see him."

"Why not? He—he hasn't got into trouble, has he?"

The detective at the other end dropped one laconic word. Even Jimmie started violently. Viv gave a little cry of genuine fear and amazement.

"Murder! Impossible. Look here, Inspector, you know Rezaire as well as I do. You know he's not on that lay."

"I don't know for certain. I admit that's not his game. But in this case… Well, he and the dead man—whom by the way is wanted too— had something in for one another."

"No. Really…"

"Anyway, we've got to pull him."

The detective asked a few more questions and then rang off. Jimmie and Viv faced one another with scared faces.

"You did damn well, Viv!" muttered Jimmie. "Why the hell they didn't come out here, I don't know—except, I suppose, they credited me with the sense not to come to you."

"But how can they have found out so soon?"

"I don't know. I locked my room and threw away the key, and no one comes in in the mornings till I ring."

"What's the jolly old row?" asked Hyslop.

"They're after Jimmie for murder."

"Good God! But…"

"Viv!" said Jimmie earnestly, "you do believe what I told you last night? I swear to God someone else shot Sam from outside,—and saved my life by it too. I'm also prepared to swear the bullet was meant for me…"

"Of course I believe," cut in the girl impatiently.

"Number One again," said Hyslop. "And I wouldn't mind betting he nipped in to see what sort of mess he'd made of you, found he'd spoiled the wrong face, had a brain-wave and faked things up to put the blame on you. How's that for a guess?"

"That's it!" cried Viv, and Jimmie agreed.

"I'll be able to clear myself in time, but it's upset my plans. They'll be watching… No, look here," he brightened with an idea. "If we can get to Victoria and hold up our gang before I'm pulled in, we can do all the explaining afterwards. It needn't stop us, after all…"

"Rather!" cried Hyslop, and was interrupted by the whirring of the telephone bell once again. "Police?" whispered Viv as she took it, adding a moment later: "No. Someone speaking French! And damn bad French… *Qui est la? Qui? Mario?…*"

Jimmie reached for the receiver, but Hyslop was before him. "'Ware traps, old boy," he said, and after listening a moment, spoke rapidly in Italian, which he knew well.

"He'll be round here in ten minutes. He rang up on his way. He says he has news,—'important, but of an importance for the Monsieur who knows about Luigi.'"

"Good," said Jimmie, biting his nails. "Wonder what the hell's up now! Are we all ready to leave for the station, H.H.? Because we may have to go quickly. I want to be there by ten."

"All ready, old son. And don't forget to take along the ticket for your suitcase in the cloakroom, in case you have to push over to France after your performin' troupe and their bit of machinery, after all."

"Right!" answered Jimmie seriously.

* * * *

Mario arrived, bristling with Italian, bad English, worse French, friendliness for Jimmie, and hatred against several unspecified enemies. When he had been calmed, he told Jimmie his story, side-tracked at intervals by expressions of delight that Jimmie had not been hurt after being drugged, and by curses directed at Neasden who, it now transpired, had knocked him down in a temper the evening before.

"I bet they were all a bit rattled in that camp yesterday," murmured Hyslop, but Jimmie signed to him not to interrupt.

Mario of course did not know the plans or aims of Number One's gang. But with the idea that they were engaged in nefarious business of some kind, and wishing for revenge, he had that morning, but an hour ago, listened at a door.

"The big man was angry…"

"Neasden?"

Mario nodded. "He was talking to the girl. There was no one else. The little M. Davis I have not seen for a day."

Jimmie smiled. He knew where the little M. Davis was. "Was Number One there?" he asked, still curious about his principal enemy.

"I do not know him. I have never seen him. But he telephoned. He was angry with Neasden, and Neasden was angry with himself. He had made some mistake, and had not found it out till very early this morning. He say, however, he will arrange the affair… Monsieur"—Mario dropped his voice—"there has been a—a murder near by. But I will help you. Neasden has—how I know not—let the police know it was you—M. Rezaire, eh?"

Jimmie nodded.

"I know. I did not do it."

Mario looked a little disappointed. His hatred of Neasden had brought about a romantic attachment for Jimmie, cemented by yesterday's munificent gift. He had almost hoped Jimmie was guilty, and that he, Mario, would be the one to save him from capture.

"But you do not know all. It is arranged—I hear it—that Neasden and the girl and the terrible Number One go to France today. From the Victoria station. They believe that you intend to be there too."

"How the devil did they know that?" ejaculated Hyslop.

"I'm beginning to think we're up against something inhuman," murmured Jimmie. "Or else infernally skillful guessing."

"So they have told the police that you seek to escape by the eleven o'clock train, and that they may catch you then. The girl spoke this on the telephone; and she said she was one of you…" Viv gave a little gasp.

"The dirty cat," she said in a most unladylike way. "As if I would ever squeak!"

"Then that's perhaps why the 'busies' aren't bothering to come round here. They're going to let me walk into the trap."

"And that, Monsieur, is all I know," finished Mario, striking an attitude.

"Well, Mario," said Jimmie seriously, "I'm very, very grateful to you. I have rewarded you…"

"Ah, yes, Monsieur; and my heart it is…"

"And I will reward you further, when I have finished with this business. You will come here in a week, and if I am not in prison, I will give you money. As for Luigi—I know no such man."

Jimmie ducked just in time to avoid a garlic-scented kiss; then Mario, dribbling grateful Italian, was shown out.

* * * *

"The devils!" said Viv, when he had gone.

But Jimmie, whose brain had been moving rapidly, was looking at his watch.

"We haven't a minute," he said swiftly. "H.H., I simply can't go to Victoria or I'll be pulled, and they'll make their get-away clean, before I can explain. Can you have a shot at the business by yourself? They don't know you. And the Yard has nothing on you that they know of. Detain the gang; fight them; make a row; accuse them of arson, or murder or whatever you like—anything to make the police intervene, and stop them catching the train. There'll be three of them, according to Mario,—Neasden, Zita and our friend the great unknown. Who'll have the Murchison, I don't know. But do your best!"

"Right. I will. But what will you do?"

Jimmie smiled. "There's a boat-train from Victoria at ten, which I can just catch. I'll be away, with luck, before the police arrive at the station. It goes by the Newhaven-Dieppe route and gets in to Paris tonight at St. Lazare, a quarter of an hour or so before the eleven o'clock Calais train gets in at the Nord. Just time for me to get across and wait at the Nord on the off chance of our friends escaping you at Victoria. Get me? I'm going to back you up in case you let anything past."

He went to the door.

"Good man!" ejaculated Hyslop.

"If you want to get in touch with me, wire the Ritzillon Hotel. And if by chance you come over, I'll leave a message there for you."

He opened the door.

"Good-bye, Jimmie!" said Viv suddenly in a small voice.

Jimmie came back and took her in his arms.

Hyslop, a nice young man, obligingly looked out of the window and announced that the coast was clear outside.

"Don't worry, Viv, my darling!" whispered Jimmie. "*I* don't, now that Sam's out of the way, and now that I've got something to come back to. And after this is over, you and I will be rolling in money and you needn't lift another fur coat as long as you live."

CHAPTER XVII

ON THE TRAIL

The Newhaven boat-train, rattling through the south of England, carried with it Jimmie Rezaire. He had obtained his ticket and suitcase at Victoria without being observed, and had then boarded the train and locked himself in the corridor lavatory till well after the start. He was now gazing out of the window with a very worried expression on his face. Though the police had been warned,—and quite correctly too, they had every reason to suppose—that he was going by the eleven o'clock, yet he credited them with sufficient sense not to relax any other precautions. Probably they were watching all the ports and stations—a poor prospect for him, for his passport obtained for him by 'Captain Smith' was of course known to them, as was his description.

He studied a time-table and found he had only twenty-one minutes between the arrival of the train at Newhaven and the departure of the boat. Could he dodge anyone waiting for him then? Almost impossible. Passengers were herded through gateways like sheep on these occasions. One detective stationed by the passport barrier would be sufficient. And, if he were stopped, twenty-one minutes were of no earthly use to him. A bare twenty-one minutes to convince a Newhaven detective that he was sufficiently innocent of a murder charge in London to be allowed to proceed on his journey out of English jurisdiction. Particularly when that murder charge had been framed up to show his guilt. It would take a week and probably a trial on top of it.

He wondered how Neasden had framed it; for there had of course been nothing about it in the papers; it had been discovered too late for the morning edition. It would have been quite easy to arrange. Probably Neasden had merely shut the window, moved the body slightly, and left the revolver which he had himself used for the deed. That, with the discovery by the police that Jimmie was the occupant under an assumed name of that bedroom at "The Vine," would be almost irrefutable evidence. In addition, the police knew well that Sam and he had quarrelled. He wiped his forehead. The more he thought about it, the more he realized that he would be lucky if he escaped at all from the web spun round him; let alone get across to France to back Hyslop up. And if he did get over—he might be wise to stay there.

He started to elaborate schemes, but could not concentrate, for, in spite of everything, his mind was really on his main plan. How had Hyslop got on at Victoria? It was past eleven now: either he had been successful or else Number One and Neasden and Zita were laughing together in a carriage as they sped to safety with the Murchison sighter. Two men had already died—four, if the airmen were included—and one was now in prison for murder, all on account of that little framework invented in a peaceful professor's workshop. It had started its career of death-dealing sooner than its inventor had reckoned, and in a much different fashion.

* * * *

The train drew into Newhaven Harbor Station and Jimmie rose with a sigh to get his suitcase from the rack. He must get across to Paris if it was humanly possible, in case Hyslop failed. He stepped out quickly onto the platform. He had a vague and slender plan—a bluff which might get him safely past the passport barrier and onto the boat.

But he was destined never to use it. For he had not taken three steps, before he was tapped on the shoulder. Turning, he saw two detectives.

"I'm Detective Inspector Worrington, and I want you, Rezaire," said the elder one shortly. "Will you come with me?"

Without a word Jimmie turned. Sick with the knowledge of his defeat and apprehensive that that defeat might become still more disastrous, he accompanied the men to a little office.

"Your pal Sam died suddenly last night, Rezaire," said the Inspector as they went. "You're wanted for it. I caution you…"

"How—how am I supposed to have done it?" asked Jimmie in a dry voice, as they entered the office; while one or two curious passengers who had followed, stopped outside to peer in through the window.

"Well, you ought to know," said the other man, younger and less discreet. "We heard you were a clever one; but why the hell you went and left your gun, silencer and all, where a child could find it…"

His superior rebuked him. "Now then, Evans, less chatter! And pull that blind down; we don't want half the station staring in!" He turned to his prisoner and continued: "You'll hear all about it at the inquest, Rezaire!"

Jimmie, however, began another question, as the detective moved to the blind.

But he never finished it. The first words had barely left his lips before a sharp snap drove the remainder from his thoughts. The blind, slipping from the careless fingers of the man at the window, had sprung up again to the top. At the sound Jimmie's mind suddenly flashed back to that terrible minute last night, when the blind of his bedroom had similarly snapped up to the roller. He heard again the "Phtt" of the silenced revolver, saw Sam's arrested hand and ghastly forehead; and, as each thought and incident of that horrible crisis stood out clear in his mind, he remembered something else. A new wild hope came to him and eager words tumbled from his lips:

"Look here," he stammered excitedly. "Inspector! Listen a moment! There's a mistake, I can't stop—I've got to catch this boat. I'm on Secret Service work—it's an international matter... I must get on..."

"You bet!" put in the younger man sarcastically.

"I'm speaking the truth. You can prove I'm on Secret Service..."

"H'm. But Secret Service work don't include murder," remarked Inspector Worrington. "At least to my knowledge."

"I did not do it, and I'm after those who did." Jimmie calmed down a bit. Excitement would not help him to make the other believe the improbable. He began to speak swiftly but with the utmost conviction he could put into his voice. He was fighting against time and the precious minutes were slipping past.

"See here, Inspector! I am supposed, am I not, to have killed the man in that room?" The detective nodded. "Well, the shot that killed him was fired from the roof outside. I saw it."

"Go *on*!" The man was sceptical but interested.

"Yes, and I shall give evidence on oath to that effect. And there will be definite proof by then of what I say. If it was fired from outside I can't have done it?"

"That'll have to be shown. Where'll your proof come from?"

"You can obtain the proof now," said Jimmie earnestly. "In fact, they may have already discovered it... Can you get through to London on the phone? Your men up there have evidently not yet noticed the bedroom blind. They will find it has a bullet hole through it from outside; but, as it snapped up with the impact, it would not be obvious. Wouldn't that explain it?"

For the first time the Inspector looked thoroughly doubtful.

"For God's sake!" cried Jimmie, "I'm only asking you to telephone to give me a chance to..."

"I've got no authority..."

"I'll stand trial, do anything you like, but help me to have a shot to get on that boat. Get permission from London for me to cross. Look here"—he played his last card—"I told you I was Secret Service in spite of this mix up. Well, I'm after the Murchison sighter."

Luckily the Detective Inspector aspired to secret work, and had bean following what he could glean of the Murchison business with the utmost interest. He, too, on his own had held the theory that it might be easily smuggled over on a Channel boat. He suddenly saw the matter in its new aspect and perceived, too, the importance of the utmost speed. And, after all, a telephone call did not commit him to anything.

He was galvanized to action; and he was an efficient man.

"It may be a plant of some kind," he said. "But I'll try it." Telling his companion to watch the prisoner closely, he ran out of the room along the platform. Jimmie and his guardian followed.

Jimmie, looking at his watch as the detective unceremoniously took charge of the station master's office, saw that they had used already twelve minutes of the precious twenty-one. Nine more minutes. Just time, with the utmost luck, and...

With a sudden sinking of the heart he realized that the whole thing was after all impossible. For Inspector Worrington might, indeed could, get London in a minute, but nobody from Scotland Yard could get round to Warsaw Street in time to verify what he said and give permission for his release. He could have wept with sudden vexation and disappointment.

As the detective took the phone up Jimmie perceived there was only one thing to do—one last chance. He must gamble on there being someone in authority actually on the scene of the murder at the moment... He reached for the telephone directory as Inspector Worrington snapped into the transmitter:

"Police speaking from Newhaven. Utmost urgency! Clear the line for London!..."

"What's that?" he wheeled round on Jimmie.

"Headquarters are no good. You must get the place itself." Jimmie's eager fingers were fluttering the directory for the telephone number of "The Vine."

"Right!" Worrington had realized. "Let me have the number... Clear that line, miss. Number required follows..."

"Thank God!" sighed Jimmie as he found it was on the phone. "Gerrard 78057. Public house called 'The Vine.'"

Rezaire had always hated detectives, but he was filled with gratitude and admiration for this one at least. For he was now heart and soul in this enterprise and showed himself a hustler of almost American training. But only seven minutes now remained.

"Gerrard 78057," he jerked out. "Police speaking. Clear that line, or the Lord have mercy on you." Over his shoulder he flung to his subordinate: "Evans! I'll watch Rezaire. Go and hold the Dieppe boat as long as you can. They'll give you three or four minutes on this tide… Now, miss, quick as quick please!" Four blessed minutes' grace. Ten altogether now. Jimmie's whole body twitched with excitement.

It was barely seventy seconds, but it seemed like an hour before the detective said:

"Is that Gerrard 78057? 'The Vine' public house? Who's speaking? Detective Inspector Worrington of Newhaven this end. That's the scene of last night's murder, isn't it, Constable? I want to talk to whoever is there on the job. Get the biggest man you can find to speak here at once… Good God! Is he?" he added a moment later, and turned to Jimmie. "Evidently Headquarters think it's something more important than an ordinary murder."

"Why?"

"Well,"—Inspector Worrington grinned—"Marden himself is actually on the spot at this moment, and the constable's gone to fetch him." Jimmie could have shouted aloud with joy. To catch one of the most prominent men in all Scotland Yard, a man who could by a word give him his release, was luck indeed.

"Yes, sir," Worrington was saying within a minute. "That's me. I have the man Rezaire here, sir—according to instructions sent round to all ports. But it seems…" He spoke rapidly for a minute, giving in curt, concise phrases the gist of Jimmie's appeal. Then he listened, spoke again, and stopped.

"He's gone to look," he said over his shoulder. "He knows something about your business, I think. The Secret Service have been talking to him. They were rather upset at this happening, because they reckoned you were on to something good and had spoiled it. They'd been on a false trail themselves in Norfolk, so Marden says. And why we… Yes, sir?" he broke off. "Very good. I'm to let him go…"

Jimmie seized his suitcase.

The Inspector put the receiver down. "Run!" he said briefly. "He's satisfied it's a frame against you. But you're wanted for the inquest, and he's putting you on your honor to come back. Now cut off!"

"You're the first detective I ever met who had real grey matter," laughed Jimmie.

Then he raced down the platform and through the barriers. He met the younger detective returning, and for a moment thought he would be stopped. But he shouted urgently that he was not escaping and was passed.

He took the gangway as a dozen lusty men were pulling it away, and arrived breathless on the deck.

Here he heard an acid old lady with a sour expression remark loudly to a companion that some Britishers would probably be late for Judgment Day from sitting drinking in depot saloons.

CHAPTER XVIII

NUMBER ONE AT LAST

Arrived at Dieppe, Jimmie passed the Customs and found a place in the train. He was still rather overcome with the wonder of his luck at Newhaven. It almost looked as though Fate had need of him in Paris.

He sat back in his corner seat wondering what had happened at Victoria and whether after all his trouble he would have anything more to do. He was inclined to believe Hyslop had not been successful; for if anything had transpired, surely Marden would have known of it when telephoning and would not have let him go across to France after all. In a way he rather hoped his companion had failed. Though Hyslop was too good a fellow to try and oust him from any praise, he wanted the credit of the capture himself. If only he had remembered that spring blind in time, and had realized how easy it would be to explain Sam's death as a frame-up, he could have gone to the police in London at once and put it right, and yet been at Victoria himself. He wondered again how Hyslop…

The name Hyslop in the ramifications of his thoughts, seemed all at once to connect with something external. He suddenly realized that a man outside on the platform was walking rapidly down the train, waving a telegram and shouting, "Meestaire Yimmee Eeslope!"

Like a flash, Rezaire leaned out and shouted: "*Hé, là bas*?"

The man stopped, looked at him and repeated the name.

"That's me!" Rezaire assured him. "Mr. Jimmie Hyslop!" He took the telegram and tipped its bearer.

Damned clever, he thought to himself, as he tore the flimsy paper open. Young Hyslop was certainly worth taking trouble over. Too cautious to address a telegram to Jimmie by name when he knew the police might be after him, he addressed it to a name he knew well would be recognized when called out, and had added to ensure this, "Passenger on the Paris boat-train, Dieppe." Jimmie read the printed words as the train steamed out.

"Controversy Victoria resulted beak pulled with typewriter full-stop one and lady unidentified and will cross safe beak saying alone."

Jimmie sat back and gave a deep sigh of relief. At last then the Murchison was in safe hands; for he realized that the words "beak pulled with typewriter" was Hyslop's way of saying that the big-nosed Neasden had been arrested with the stolen sighter on him. The remainder of the message, however, was not so promising, for it indicated that the slippery Number One had escaped unobserved and Zita with him; nor would they be caught at Dover since the police now had what they were after, and Neasden had evidently persuaded them that he was alone, in order to insure his companions' escape.

Number One then had been worsted again. He had lost another of his gang and his prize as well. But he himself and the girl had escaped. Jimmie wondered if he could still get hold of him in Paris. Unfortunately things were different now, for they were on foreign soil. To secure his arrest, Number One would have to be brought back to England; which would be an impossible business. One could not, working alone in a strange country, forcibly kidnap a clever and ruthless man; and it would have to be a very subtle ruse indeed that would result in his being enticed back of his own free will.

Jimmie sighed regretfully. Even though the balance of the honors rested with him, it looked as though the game were finished at last. It was no use going to the Nord Station after all; except perhaps to try and secure a glimpse at any rate of his hitherto invisible and powerful opponent.

And that might be dangerous. Number One had a big score against him.

* * * *

By the time the train drew in at the St. Lazare Station, Jimmie had decided to dismiss all thoughts of spies and stolen secrets from his mind and to stay the night in Paris by way of a pleasant holiday after all he had undergone, returning to London at his ease next day. With this idea he gave his bag to a porter and named his favorite hotel. He began to think of Montagne's—for Jimmie knew how to eat well and enjoyed eating.

Two minutes later he changed his mind absolutely. For as he reached the end of the platform he encountered an employee of Thomas Cook & Son's, who stood there scrutinizing the passengers and saying interrogatively as they passed: "Monsieur Rezaire? Monsieur Rezaire?"

"Yes? You want me?" said Jimmie eagerly. Without doubt this was Hyslop again, and he began to feel that life was about to become exciting once more.

"You are Monsieur Rezaire?" The man held out an envelope. "Here is a message for you. It has been telephoned from London to our office but an hour ago with instructions to catch you as you left this train."

Jimmie snatched at it, for the second time blessing Hyslop's ingenuity that despised time and space. It began:

"Bearer is promised a hundred francs for safe delivery. Please pay him." Hyslop evidently was taking no chances of missing Jimmie through insufficient search. Jimmie smiled and read on: "Neasden's typewriter just discovered by experts to be sham, designed in case of capture to ensure One's escape with real goods. Business therefore now in your hands as prearranged…"

Jimmie was galvanized to instant action. He thrust about a hundred and twenty francs into the astonished employee's hand and shouted to his porter: "A taxi for the *Gare du Nord*! The quickest one in Paris!"

He departed from the station in a breathless hooting and whirring of wheels, leaving the porter fingering a ten franc note and staring at his compatriot from Cook's. Both were now quite convinced that all Englishmen were mad.

* * * *

Jimmie's lavish tip had been noticed by the taxi-driver, who excelled himself even in such a city of furious driving as Paris. Five full minutes remained to Jimmie when his taxi drew up outside the Nord Station; and a hurried question to an official doubled his margin of time, as he learned the boat-train would be five minutes late, for which occurrence the taxi-driver, an opportunist, seemed inclined to take credit.

Jimmie, amused, studied the man closely and decided to use him further. He began by giving him fifty francs and asking him to do a favor. The driver instantly expressed his willingness to break the law in ten different ways in return for such munificence.

"I am going to leave my suitcase in your car," began Jimmie in his voluble and almost perfect French. "I want you to wait here with your engine running. I am going to meet two friends, a man and a girl, by the English train, but,—this is important,—I do not want them to see me. So I shall follow them out at a distance and you must watch for me, to indicate them to you. After which you will follow their taxi to any hotel. But discreetly—so discreetly! It is understood?"

"*Absolument, monsieur.*"

"For you there will be another fifty francs—afterwards."

The man brushed this aside—nominally. He was quite eager to assist in this matter. With true Gallic instinct he had plumbed its meaning. Obviously it concerned itself with a deserted husband who was about to catch the runaway pair. What more could life offer? To show his anxiety to be on Jimmie's side he said:

"Monsieur will take the number of my cab and licence, then I shall not run away meanwhile with Monsieur's valise?"

"Monsieur has taken it already," remarked Jimmie briefly as he disappeared into the station.

The man only grinned. He realized that this was no "*poire*" he had to deal with. He felt sorry for that other who had stolen away the wife.

* * * *

The Calais train hissed in and disgorged its passengers. Jimmie had hidden himself behind a pillar whence he could observe the end of the platform. He had not been able to disguise himself at all and so did not want to be seen; but he was taking a chance on the pair having relaxed their vigilance by now, since they knew that in all probability their chief opponent was out of the way and that Neasden's capture and ruse had taken suspicion away from them. At the same time, Jimmie was anxious. He had a difficult task before him, for he did not know anything at all about Number One and was relying on the simple fact that Zita would be with him and that he would recognize her.

The passengers swept past unendingly and then suddenly he saw the girl. She was chatting quite unconcernedly to a companion and was not even bothering to look about her. Jimmie craned forward and saw at last—Number One.

A thin wiry man with a broad forehead, pale almost invisible eyebrows and black deep-set eyes. The chin was pointed and the mouth was hard and firm with thin clean-shaven lips. For a moment the shape of the nose seemed to stir some memory in Jimmie's mind; then he realized he had never seen the fellow before. And this was the redoubtable Number One.

Jimmie followed them out with caution. The man was carrying two suitcases, one of which seemed heavier than the other; and he would not allow a porter to take them. Without doubt one held the precious Murchison, and Jimmie drew his breath in with excitement.

He caught sight of his own taxi-driver, waiting in suppressed excitement, and a nod of the head indicated the pair as they got into a taxi a short distance away. They drove off, and at a discreet interval Jimmie followed.

Number One evidently had now a clear conscience, for his taxi made straight for the Rue de Richelieu and stopped outside one of the tall old Paris houses of that neighborhood, now converted into a small hotel, providing good rooms but no meals.

Jimmie halted his taxi higher up. When he had seen the others enter, he got out, paid off his man and stood on the pavement to collect his thoughts.

This then was "the usual hotel" to which Number One had referred and in which Siminski was presumably already installed. By now the two spies from England had met their Russian accomplice. The problem that confronted him now was how to get into that hotel, the Hotel Metz, abstract the Murchison sighter and get back to England with it.

He turned at last with his bag and walked slowly away in search of a shop at the back of the Palais Royal. Here he had a friend who specialized in disguises and who had been useful to him on one or two previous occasions.

Half an hour later, a dapper little Frenchman, who had, he confessed with shame, been out of France for four years learning to speak the English—that damnable language which twists the throat, so that afterwards almost is one unable to manage one's native tongue—was talking to the equally communicative manager of the Hotel Metz. He engaged a room in the name of Monsieur Jules and he talked, how he talked. About his beloved Paris, the beautiful city he was so pleased to see again. About the theatres,—what were they like now? About the restaurants? And about the adorable *cocottes* than whom no city possessed better? *Ma foi*—he kissed his hand—they would welcome him tonight! But—he became confidential and leaned over the bureau on which conveniently lay the hotel register with the room numbers—one had told him that the pretty *poules* all had such expensive ideas nowadays; their heads had been turned by these so rich foreigners with whom, one said, Paris was over-run. Was this true? Were there actually foreigners, English and American, in this very hotel? Germans and Italians too? Russians he did not mind...

After a quarter of an hour he seemed to recollect that he had engaged a room and was shown upstairs. He and the manager bowed at one another with every protestation of good faith, and then he shut the door.

When he had locked it he sat on the bed and laughed silently to himself in a very English manner. The voluble manager, all unwittingly, had been exceedingly helpful about foreigners. A Mr. Jones of Bristol was in the hotel and had been for ten days; but he was of no use to Jimmie. A Monsieur Petroff from Russia, who had come, so his labels denoted, by air, had arrived the evening before. This was better; it could be no other than Siminski. And finally, a Mr. and Mrs. Layman of London had but recently arrived...

"Number One and Zita!" murmured Jimmie to himself and added piously: "I hope they really are married. But at least it means only one room instead of two for me to get into tonight."

* * * *

In spite of his disguise, which was effective though light, Jimmie did not dare risk an encounter on the stairs with Number One. He had too high an opinion of the other's cleverness. So after a few minutes, spent in examining the room and particularly the window which had a small balcony, he slipped out, crossed the road to a small Cafe-Bar opposite and established himself in a position which guarded the hotel door.

He had not been any too quick. In about five minutes he saw Zita emerge, followed by Number One's wiry little figure and then by a tall, stooping pale figure,—Siminski the Russian without a doubt—a man as unlike a spy as anyone Jimmie had ever seen. A moment later, however, he admitted that to be unlike a spy was very probably to be a good spy.

Well, he ruminated, as they vanished towards the Avenue de l'Opera, he had got a line on all three of them now. Tonight he ought to be able to get his hands on the Murchison at last. He felt highly pleased with himself; and for the first time realized that after all the rush and excitement he was tired and hungry.

He finished his drink and was about to leave, when a sudden thought struck him. The spies must be hungry too; they had almost certainly gone out to a restaurant. Therefore they would be away for an hour at least. *Now*, not tonight, was his real opportunity. He could slip back to the hotel, snap up the Murchison sighter and catch the night train for London. There was no doubt that that was his best course.

He gave the three spies a couple more minutes and then strolled across to the hotel. It looked almost too easy; his enemies, believing him under lock and key in England, had shown themselves completely off their guard. How Hyslop would have liked to have been in on this final triumph!

It struck him at this point that there was just a chance that the young man had come over by airplane that afternoon to lend him a hand. In which case he would have gone to the Ritzillon Hotel to get in touch. Jimmie paused with his foot on the first stair and turned back to the telephone by the salon.

No, the clerk at the Ritzillon assured him over the wire, Monsieur Hyslop had not been heard of. Was he coming? In that case could one give a message?

But certainly. If they would be so good as to put a note up for him against his arrival to let him know that a Monsieur Jules had called up from the Hotel Metz. Monsieur Hyslop would no doubt arrive soon. What? They would be delighted. Good!

Jimmie rang off. In another moment he had obtained, unobserved from the board, the key of Number One's room—the number of which he had noted earlier while leaning over the bureau conversing with the proprietor—and was speeding upstairs.

Incautious fool, thought Jimmie, on finding the door was not locked. He made a rapid search of the room, but could not discover the little piece of machinery that meant so much to him. In one of the two half-unpacked suitcases, however,—that containing the man's clothes,—he found proof that it had been brought; for there were several crumpled sheets of newspaper which smelled faintly of oily metal, and had without doubt been used to wrap it up.

He searched again in every drawer and cupboard, and swore. Then he swore at his own foolishness. Of course, it had already been passed to Siminski; they were glad enough no doubt to get rid of it. Luckily he had also ascertained at the same time the number of the Russian's room, in case it was needed.

Siminski's door, however, was locked—a sign, Rezaire hoped, that what he sought was inside—and this necessitated another excursion to the board in the hall for the key. On his way up again he had to dodge a chambermaid on the first floor, but at last found himself in Siminski's bedroom.

In a few minutes his search was successful. Under a muffler in a wardrobe drawer he came upon the Murchison sighter for which so many men had risked so much. It was just a framework of aluminum with a slightly damaged appearance, due to its fall. Two little bent levers projected from it, with a broken end of electric cable, and there was a small aluminum sphere with a fragment of graticulated glass lens still embedded in the center.

His eager fingers were on it, when a voice said in perfect English, from behind him:

"Your hands up, if you please!"

At the door which he held closed behind him stood Siminski, the pale stooping Russian.

"Though I have not the pleasure of your acquaintance," he continued mockingly, "I presume you are Mr. Jimmie Rezaire. Having but recently read a most communicative paragraph in the newspaper, we rather thought we might find you here after all."

CHAPTER XIX

THE UNKNOWN REVEALED

"Turn your back!" commanded the Russian, as Jimmie's hands reluctantly went over his head. Jimmie obeyed, and felt the muzzle of the automatic at his spine, while the other took his revolver from his pocket.

In a few moments he was lying on the floor, as skillfully gagged and roped up as he had ever been by a single handed man in all his life. He felt at once that he would not be able to get out of those bonds if he tried for hours.

Siminski gave a few final tugs, and got to his feet. He then examined the fastenings of the window with great care. Next, after re-shutting the drawer which contained the Murchison, he rolled Jimmie contemptuously under the bed.

At the door he paused. "I am going to resume my interrupted dinner with my friends," he said; then added sarcastically: "And they told me you had a reputation for being clever."

Jimmie heard the key turn in the lock, and knew that this time it would not go back on the board in the hall. Nor could he move legs or arms an inch to make a noise and attract attention. He was as helpless and inert as a felled tree.

He lay there cursing his ill-luck and his foolish lack of precaution. Siminski had been right; he had been caught like any novice. He cursed, too, the inquisitive reporter or the talkative constable who had thus given the hint to his enemies through the papers that he had not been safely arrested in England after all. It had not taken them long to surmise that he might be yet on their tracks.

And now this was the finish. He was done for. He would never catch that night train. Fear leaped at him in the darkness. Would he ever catch a train at all? He almost screamed into his gag in sudden panic. Surely Number One, now that he was safe and out of England, would spare his life?

It seemed hours that he lay there in the stuffy, dusty darkness under the enormous bed. At one time he heard a clock strike nine. Was it only a bare three hours ago that he had driven up to the Gare du Nord and made the little plot with his genial taxi-driver?

At about ten o'clock Siminski reentered. He had obviously been celebrating Number One's success, and so too had Zita, who followed. They were laughing together and the Russian's body stooped even more as he whispered something into Zita's ear. Number One himself, however, entering a moment later, looked as cool as ever, and his deep black eyes were just as cold and calculating, as when Jimmie had seen him on the platform.

Siminski, whose breath smelled of brandy, had by then pulled his prisoner blinking out into the light with a flourish.

"Here you are, Viloff!" he said. "*Here's* the rat!"

Number One, who at last had a name, stood looking down on the bound figure of his enemy with calm triumph. At first sight he had given a start of surprise, but then he bent down closer and his keen gaze penetrated the disguise Jimmie still wore.

"So we meet again," he said softly, and released the gag.

Jimmie stared. He felt he knew the voice. Where had he heard it before? Surely it could not be...

"I think our last encounter was in Piccadilly Circus. By luck I had happened to see you in Whitehall—soon after you got your passport, as I subsequently ascertained—and that made me realize—for the first time I admit—that you were working for the Secret Service."

Jimmie gasped. He recognized Number One at last. Fool that he had been! Add to this man Viloff a padding of stomach, bushy eyebrows and a beard, grey pince-nez to conceal those remarkable eyes, give him a puffy method of speaking broken English, and he was Monsieur Villon, proprietor of the *Coin de Paradis* restaurant.

"Monsieur Villon!" Jimmie ejaculated incredulously.

"The same," smiled the other and puffed suddenly, "*Que voulez vous?*"

He turned and spoke rapidly to Siminski in Russian while Jimmie preserved a desperately mortified silence. How inconceivably dense he with his vaunted cleverness had been not to guess! Why, the man had played off one of his own old tricks on him. A favorite argument of Jimmie's was that the stupid criminal always committed his crime first and disguised himself afterwards, thus increasing his chances of being taken, while the clever criminal disguised himself for his crime and afterwards became himself once more, leaving the police looking for a non-existent man probably in disguise. Why, he saw it all now, the whole of the *Coin de Paradis* was a disguise—and a proper working one at that—bought up, lock, stock and barrel, by Number One, to cover the headquarters of a most dangerous spy gang. And he, Rezaire, had been fooled like any schoolboy. How Neasden must have laughed to himself when Jimmie kept asking who Number One was and yet a moment later spoke innocently of "the proprietor!"... Number One—Viloff—was talking in English again, and now his voice was hard, metallic, like his dark black eyes.

"I have a score to settle with you, Mr. Rezaire. You have caused me infinite trouble. You have landed two of my party in prison, you have put me to great expense—in fact, I'm not sure you haven't driven me out of business. How you have done this, working more or less alone, I cannot understand." Jimmie cast his eyes down lest the other should read in them the knowledge that he had Hyslop as a confederate. "It shows that though you have done foolish things, you must be really clever, because I myself am no child. Of course," continued Viloff thoughtfully, "you may have an accomplice in Shrewsbury Mansions, but I hadn't time to ascertain. Anyway, Shrewsbury Mansions are not in Paris. Really, I ought to have solved your game before, I suppose. I should have put you quietly out of the way when you were in our power, but I confess your extremely quick change from convict to—er—detective misled me into thinking you were just a criminal with no sense of loyalty towards his employer."

Still Jimmie did not speak; there was nothing to say. The other's half-cold, half-friendly way of talking had at first given him hope. Now it began to fill him with an apprehension, which at the next words kindled to his previous panic once again.

"Well, it is getting late. I think you had better say your prayers; because I don't imagine you will see tomorrow. You had better say them to this," he chuckled, and taking the Murchison sighter from the drawer, he placed it on a chair in front of Jimmie.

"An ingenious toy. I wish I could have understood it and it would have saved all this bother. However, our friends in Russia will make light of it, won't they?" he added, turning to Siminski, who, sitting on a settee talking in low tones to Zita, merely grunted in answer.

"What are you going to do with me?" asked Jimmie with dry lips.

The other answered as if he were discussing a visit to a theatre.

"Kill you, of course. There are many ways. Which would you prefer? I don't mind obliging you if it can be managed, because you have made me laugh once or twice—particularly with the little note you sent me last night by my taxi-driver."

Jimmie suddenly strained at his bonds in an access of terror and Viloff laughed easily and naturally.

"What! No preference? You leave it to me? Well, I'll fix it. Will you tell me the number of your room; for I presume you are staying in this hotel under a false name? You see I must just arrange your things there for the little drama I have in mind. Dear me! To think that in a few days' time the body of yet another unknown Englishman will be fished out of the poor old Seine. Poking his nose where it wasn't wanted, they will say. And they'll be right."

Blindly Jimmie told him the number, and Viloff passed out of sight behind his head to the door. Jimmie heard him interrupt Siminski's muttered conversation to say calmly:

"Keep an eye on him, and if he tries to shout, just choke him a bit!"

He heard Siminski's careless assent, and the gentle closing of the door.

* * * *

It was about ten minutes later that the door opened again. Jimmie heard Zita begin: "Have you fixed…" and then break off with a little cry of fear. Simultaneously he heard an exclamation of rage from Siminski and then, with an infinite gratitude, a well-known voice.

"Frightfully sorry to interrupt and all that don't you know." Again Hyslop had come to his aid.

"What do you want?" began the Russian and his words were thick, either with drink or fear.

"Careful, old love," came Hyslop's cheerful tones. "Don't move suddenly like that. I'm not frightfully good at guns and things, and this one might go shoot-bang-fire and you'd be pop-bang-dead. Just unleash my old school-chum on the floor, will you, there's a good chap, while I watch this trigger."

Jimmie, freed by the cursing Siminski, stood up and rubbed his stiff limbs. Hyslop, with a revolver in one hand and a light mackintosh over the other, was standing by the door.

"What do you imagine you're doing?" asked Zita scornfully. "And who are you?"

"Ah, you don't remember me. And it was I who made a disgustin' exhibition of myself in a public place in front of you."

Zita could do nothing but preserve an angry silence. Then Jimmie saw her eyes fall to a bag on the table beside her. He slipped out a hand just before hers, and threw the bag with the little revolver it contained to the top of the wardrobe.

"Clever!" sneered the girl with cold fury in her voice. "But just you wait…"

"I will. But don't look so hopeful, either of you," put in Hyslop as Jimmie moved to his side by the door. "Because there's not an earthly chance of your other little playmate coming in suddenly behind me. He's lying bottom up—pardon the vulgarity—on a bed wrapped round and round with all the jolly old sheets in the room. And…"

Siminski, who had been till then standing with his hands raised in the center of the room under the electric light, swaying unsteadily, suddenly made an upward grab at the globe. There sounded a small crash and the room was in darkness. Instantly there was a smart scuffle. Someone caught Jimmie's leg; but he kicked out viciously, all the concentrated energy of the last five hours in his foot, and the hold fell away. He heard Zita give a sudden short cry of pain, and muttered, "Serve her right for mixing in this!" as he made for the door. He was barely outside, before Hyslop also darted swiftly through, still with his revolver and the mackintosh over his arm and looking as cool as ever. Jimmie slammed and locked the door, as hands caught at it on the far side.

"Quick! Away!" muttered Hyslop. "Before they rouse the place!"

They sped downstairs, passing a scared chambermaid, and out into the street. Not till they had rounded three corners and were safe in a taxi did they speak.

Then Jimmie said breathlessly:

"Well, H.H., I can't thank you enough. But how the merry hell did you get there? That sort of lucky arrival usually only happens in cheap detective novels."

"Just thought you might want little Henry's help," returned the young man airily. "You got my messages?"

"Yes. Many thanks. Neasden's pulled in, I gather?"

"He is, but what the artful old devil had with him was a bit of machinery faked up to look like the Murchison. It wasn't spotted till one o'clock—or we might have done something at Dover. Clever devils! Moment I heard that, I caught the afternoon boat, arrived here at nine and went to the Ritzillon where I got a message from a Monsieur Jules at the Hotel Metz. That gave me the clue to your whereabouts."

"My God, what a fluke! I very nearly didn't bother to phone. I thought I had the whole game in my hands."

"H'm! That *was* luck. Well, I tottered out to your hotel, engaged a room by way of precaution, found yours, and sat there waiting for my friend Monsieur Jules. When you hadn't turned up by a quarter past ten I got a bit worried, and so luckily I was just nicely ready when that bird hopped in on me. He *was* surprised. From him, after an argument which left him all tied up, I gathered you'd been copped. So I nipped off to find you and did some rough stuff on my own… Who was the chappie, by the way? He seemed a pleasant-spoken bloke."

"The fellow you tied up," said Jimmie with a grin, "was Number One…"

"Gosh!" cried Hyslop. "And I never even pushed his face in..."

"Alias Viloff, alias Monsieur Villon!"

"Well, I'm all shattered," murmured Hyslop and lay back silent against the taxi cushions.

"So was I."

"Look here, where are we going?"

"Small hotel I know in Montmartre," replied Jimmie. "We'll walk the last part, to put anyone off the scent. There's no train now tonight... Good Lord!" he broke off in the utmost dismay, and buried his face in his hands.

"What's up?"

"The Murchison sighter! We've failed after all! We—never took it in the excitement. After all this..."

"Steady, old boy!" Hyslop pulled aside the mackintosh still hanging over his arm and displayed the metal frame-work bulging in a large pocket. "Here it is! I saw it sitting in a chair and snooped it in the dark."

CHAPTER XX

MOVE AND COUNTER-MOVE

Safe at last in an obscure hotel near the Place Blanche, Hyslop and Jimmie discussed plans.

"There's a ten o'clock train tomorrow reaching London five-fifteen," announced Hyslop from a time-table. "I think that'll be ours. I'm all for getting out of this gay city."

"I wish," said Jimmie, who had been lost in thought for some while, "we could have collared Viloff."

"Can't, unless we get him back to England. And that's practically imposs', unless he comes of his own free will. Which he won't."

"I wonder," said Jimmie. "You know, we've got a good bait to tempt him in this sighter. I certainly don't think he's given up heart yet. In fact, I wouldn't mind betting he'll have us trailed at all stations tomorrow." He paused, then added with deliberation: "H.H., I'm going to assume we shall see more of him and lay plans accordingly. I'm going to get that blighter…"

They talked a little more and then went to bed.

* * * *

Jimmie was up early the next day in furtherance of his new scheme. He went out into the Boulevard Clichy and made several purchases, including two cheap suitcases, with which he returned to the hotel. On his journey he had a feeling that he had been followed and verified it a moment later from a window.

"They're on to us," he remarked to Hyslop. "What a wonder Viloff is!… I believe he'd trail a soul into Hell… What's the time? Nine? Right! Well, I'm going to start the ball rolling. You know where to meet me?"

"Nine-fifty-nine at the Nord Station for the ten o'clock train. With my little bag!"

"Mind you don't put anything valuable inside," grinned Jimmie. "I'm betting you don't get on the train with it."

"Bet you a level bob I do. Unless I'm sandbagged."

"I'll take you. You've got a lot to learn before you're up to Number One's standard—or mine! Well, I'm off. So long."

"Good luck!"

Jimmie sent a man out to fetch a taxi and bring it to the hotel. Into this he put one of the suitcases—Hyslop had the other—and a large brown-paper parcel. Then he ordered the driver to go to St. Lazare Station. Out of the corner of his eye, he saw a well dressed man, apparently idling near by, hail another taxi and follow. Half-way to St. Lazare, Jimmie cried to his driver: "I meant the *Gare du Nord*. And as quick as hell! Fifty francs."

The driver went round a side turning on two wheels and was off at fifty francs' worth of high speed. For the second time in twenty-four hours, Jimmie found himself racing to the Nord Station.

Looking back through the window, he saw that he had not thrown the other taxi off, though he had gained an enormous lead by his maneuver. He did not, however, worry; for he had allowed for that.

He whirled up to the Nord, paid his man and was inside like a flash. At the first baggage depository he came to he checked in his suitcase; then he hurried across to the far side of the station, and checked the brown-paper parcel into the other *consigne*. After this he retired to the waiting-room, ostensibly to wash his hands, but while in the cubicle he took the opportunity to place one of the luggage checks in his sock and the other in his pocket-book.

Finally he strolled out mopping his forehead. About the first person he saw was the well-dressed stranger, who had followed him, and who was now anxiously looking round, obviously worried at having lost his quarry.

His face brightened as he saw Jimmie, and he hurriedly turned away. Jimmie also turned away, to hide a smile, and then went to buy his ticket.

Later, Jimmie Rezaire sauntered out of the station. He was in no great hurry. He was allowing the spy to make his own deductions as to what had happened when a man arrived at a station with luggage and then came out without it. He looked at his watch. Nine-thirty; he still had half an hour.

For a moment he paused outside lighting a cigarette; then suddenly he hailed a taxi and jumped in, directing the driver to go quickly to St. Lazare Station. To leave his inquisitive follower behind at the Nord was perhaps a bit risky he knew, but he was relying on the officialdom of the French *Consigne* authorities not to give away anything, even information. He was pleased, however, to note that the other had not considered this opportunity, for he also jumped in a taxi and followed behind.

Jimmie soon corrected his order to go to St. Lazare Station, and instead drove round the Grand Boulevards. At the end he gave his discreet watcher a great shock by going down the Rue de Richelieu and stopping, out of sheer deviltry, at the Hotel Metz as if about to get out, before telling his man to go back to the Gare du Nord.

He had judged it all well and arrived at five minutes to ten. He had barely got inside the thronged and echoing station, before a man jostled him as he passed an angle of wall. A second man was instantly at his side, and before he had realized what had happened he had been backed up into the half-hidden angle with the two men facing him as if in friendly conversation.

But this was no friendly conversation; for one of the men was Viloff, and the other held concealed a knife, the point of which Jimmie felt at his ribs.

"Your pocket-book quick!" snapped Viloff, his deep-set eyes blazing, "and look as if you were doing it in the ordinary course of a talk."

Jimmie, amazed beyond belief at the audacity of the attack, reluctantly drew out his pocket-book, and handed it over without a word.

With a smile of triumph, the other opened it and abstracted the baggage-check of the *consigne*.

"Thank you," he said mockingly.

"You've won at the last then," snarled Jimmie.

"I'm afraid so. But there's no time to kill you here. Besides, I honestly think it would be a pity. You're a worthy opponent—really you've made me stretch myself. But don't cross my road again. You can go to England now, and *bon voyage!*"

Jimmie, released, hurried through the barrier on to the platform and went up the far end of the train. With a quick glance behind him, he hailed a porter and drawing from inside his sock the other cloak-room check, handed it to the man.

"Bring me my suitcase at once, before the train goes, and there's twenty francs for you."

"*Bien, monsieur.*" The man was off at a run.

A minute or so later, as the whistle blew, the porter arrived breathless and thrust the suitcase at Jimmie, leaning out of his window. As Rezaire handed over the note, he again looked swiftly round and saw that, as he anticipated, no one had followed or noticed the man, an ordinary blue-bloused porter among many, carrying an ordinary brown suitcase among many. His ruse had come off.

Ten minutes later, while the train clanked across the northern suburbs of Paris, Hyslop dropped wearily into the seat beside him and whispered:

"You win your bob. I got in a scrimmage at the barrier and lost my bag. How the hell it went, I don't know. I hadn't time to do anything except catch this train."

"Hard lines," smiled Jimmie. "I've got mine, but in spite of all my trouble, they've got the parcel I left at the *consigne*."

Hyslop grinned back at him. "It worked then?"

"Yes. I wonder what Viloff will say when he unwraps a bird-cage with a nice heavy brick in it. And," he added reminiscently, leaning back luxuriously in his seat, "there was a note tied on to it as well. '*Un coin de Paradis pour vous*' I think it read."

* * * *

After half an hour or so, Jimmie got up and beckoned Hyslop into the corridor.

"Keep an eye on my case," he murmured. "I'm just going down the train to see whether Viloff has got on board after all."

"Good Lord, do you think he has? I was thinking this would finish him."

"I don't, though it probably took him too long to find out he'd been done, there's just a chance. But I'm going to make certain. Nothing must slip now."

"I hope to the devil he hasn't." Hyslop looked worried.

"I hope to the devil he has," grinned Jimmie surprisingly.

"Golly! You aren't half asking for it, old love."

"It'll mean something more to me than the mere money I'll get if I can land old Viloff safe in an English prison. In fact, that's what I'm playing for," he added as he started along the swaying train.

* * * *

"Not a soul," he announced to his waiting companion. "But I shouldn't be surprised if we see him at Calais yet. A fast car could do it."

"I wonder just what his little game will be in that case," murmured Hyslop.

"Whatever it is, I wonder if mine won't be better," retorted Jimmie.

CHAPTER XXI

THE LAST ROUND

Jimmie carried the precious suitcase in his right hand and Hyslop kept close to his right side, so that the bag was between them, as they moved from the train towards the Calais boat. Already that day each of them had been held up in the midst of a crowd in broad daylight, and they were taking no chances.

On this occasion, however, no one attempted to wrest the bag away from them, no one even looked at all suspicious. Hyslop took this as proof that they had won through, but Jimmie thought otherwise. He knew his man too well by now, and he gave him credit for realizing that he could not stick his enemy up in a public place twice in one morning. At the same time, he was now certain that Viloff had not relinquished the chase; for he had caught a glimpse of a powerful dust-covered car, with a chauffeur at the wheel, standing outside the station. From an official he had gleaned that it belonged to some fool who had missed the train at Paris—probably, his informant added, an American, for who else would care so little for money as to waste a ticket and hire a car, or who else would be in such a hurry?

Viloff, then, was at hand, Jimmie realized. He might even be a passenger on the boat if he were bold enough to risk a temporary return to England in order to achieve his object. Again Jimmie hoped he would. If he did, Jimmie was going to ensure that his return was not at all temporary.

On embarkation, the pair instantly went down below and Rezaire at once secured a life-belt jacket, for he was at all times nervous and on this occasion in particular thought it quite probable that he might find himself in the water before the end of the journey. A quick push in mid-Channel was not so difficult for a clever man like Viloff; and he realized fully by now that his opponent had some deep scheme in hand, which probably he would trust to no one else. Jimmie wondered what it was.

Leaving Hyslop to stroll round the ship and see if he could spot Viloff, Jimmie went below and adjusted his life-belt in an empty corner of the men's saloon. Then, still carrying the precious suitcase, which had not yet left his side, he came on deck. The passengers displayed amusement at his appearance, belted and bag in hand; but Jimmie did not mind.

The gangways were at last cast off; the steamer's whistle sounded and she moved slowly forward. Hyslop came up to Jimmie and reported that he had not seen their enemy. He was still inclined to think the other had given up. But, with the evidence of the motor car, Jimmie knew better. Viloff had come on board early and concealed himself, planning no doubt some last desperate effort. This in a way was good news; for it meant that, unless Viloff jumped overboard, he was now definitely en route for England and the hands of the police. The man was taking an enormous risk. What could he have in his mind? Jimmie, the suitcase gripped tight in his hand, continually looked about him.

The boat moved slowly out of Calais, passing impassive rows of fishermen on the walls and jetties. Suddenly there was a stir among those passengers at the forward end of the deck. Something was happening ahead. The siren let forth angry blasts. People surged to the rails and curiously Jimmie went with them, though he kept firm hold of his bag. Standing on his toes he sought the interruption.

Directly ahead in the track of the steamer he saw was a motor-launch. Apparently it was out of control, for it was going round in circles, while the two people who occupied it were frantically straining at something near to the engine. The big steamer with imperious whistle blasts drew inexorably nearer, though the engines were now stopped. At one moment it looked as though the little craft would be run down, then a wave seemed to catch it, drawing it just aside from the overhanging bows.

Everyone, even Jimmie, was staring over the side at the launch now so close to them, while the captain was wiping his forehead and shouting abuse from above. Looking down on the occupants of the launch, as it swept past, Rezaire suddenly recognized the pallid, upturned face of Siminski.

At that very moment, a sudden violent push in the back made him stagger and clutch the rail with both hands. He recovered his balance in an instant; as he did so there was a shout from two or three bystanders and a loud splash. Whirling round, Jimmie found Number One's deep cold eyes blazing straight into his own. And the suitcase was gone.

No one had seen Viloff slip up from a companionway and in the excitement quietly loop a life-belt round the handle of Jimmie's bag, then pushing him abruptly aside, slide it overboard between the rails. But for the fact that Hyslop at the last moment had gripped his arm, the spy himself would no doubt have followed the bag, to swim to the safety of the launch. As it was, foiled in this part of his plan, he at once began to play a part.

"I am so sorry, sir," he apologized in heartbroken tones, as the passengers crowded round. "It caught my foot. I cannot sufficiently assure you..."

Jimmie set his teeth. "It is nothing," he said curtly.

"It's all right," cried a man. "That launch has picked it up."

"Looks as though a life-belt got entangled round it, and it floated," said another. "Certainly, a bit of luck."

For a moment an intense triumph shone in Viloff's eyes, then he was continuing in a meek, pleasant voice:

"I am desolated. I do not know what to say. Perhaps it will be restored. I will write to the authorities, on arrival. In the meanwhile..." Mechanically Jimmie gazed after the launch, which was now, amid murmurs of surprise from the passengers, running very swiftly and in complete control westward along the coast. It was making, Jimmie knew well, for some prearranged landing, where the car would pick up its occupants before officials could get there. Up above, the captain was impervious to suggestions. He had but one job—to get his boat to Dover. For him the incident was closed.

"If," Viloff was continuing politely, "I can repair any loss—here is my card!"

With a faint smile, Jimmie took the offered pasteboard and read:

MONSIEUR L. VILLON
Restaurateur
Coin de Paradis Restaurant,
Warsaw Street, London

He saw the other's lips move soundlessly in the words "*Que voulez vous?*..."

* * * *

"Well, I'm damned!" said Hyslop, when Viloff raised his hat and departed and an elderly colonel had finished assuring Jimmie that if he sent a wireless to Calais the authorities would surely obtain and forward on his bag. "Well, I'm damned!"

"Wasn't it neat?" said Jimmie in reluctant praise. "Tying on the life-belt, too, to make it float long enough for Siminski to pick up. That man's got a head on him and no mistake."

"Where are you going now?" asked Hyslop, as the other moved off.

"To send a wireless..."

"But, my dear old chappie, you aren't such a mug as to think..."

"To Dover, asking for a couple of detectives to meet this boat."

"Oh, I see... But will they do it?"

"Yes. You bet we're in good now, after catching Davis and Neasden. Anyway, I'll sign it 'Inspector Gullidge' so they can phone him for reference if they like."

"Well, even though Zita and the Russian have got away with the suitcase, we'll have old Viloff at last?"

"Perhaps," said Jimmie soberly. "Perhaps not. You'd better run off and trail him now till we get in."

* * * *

They had delayed too long. Hyslop could not find his quarry. He and Jimmie spent the rest of the trip trying to locate the spy's hiding place on board, and failed. The man had disappeared, as completely as if he had gone overboard. Jimmie began to wonder seriously whether he hadn't dropped into the water, after all.

At Dover, two detectives appeared and under Jimmie's supervision watched the passengers off, but there was no sign of the wanted man. Then they combed the ship out in the gathering dusk, but except for the crew and a few porters with belated luggage, there was not a soul.

The detectives began to get sarcastic, Jimmie angry and puzzled.

"He didn't come off, I'm certain; so he's on the ship somewhere."

"Nothing to do but to search her again," said one of the police officials. "All cabins, stokehold, forecastle, and so on."

"His game should be to…" began the other, when with a sudden cry, Jimmie sprang forward.

A sailor, carrying a bag apparently left behind by some passenger, was just passing; and it was at him Jimmie sprang.

In a minute they had secured Viloff, spitting curses, Viloff in full sailor's kit, stolen or bribed from one of the many harbor porters.

"By Heaven! Five seconds more and he'd have been past us."

"And we were watching passengers," murmured a detective, snapping on handcuffs…

"At last," said Jimmie…

"Well," said Viloff, calming down, "I must admit it's your turn for a bit of luck. You may have got me, but you haven't beaten me. There's one thing you've lost."

"Oh, by the way," said Jimmie coolly, "that reminds me. I meant to tell you before, but you were so busy apologizing I didn't get a chance. The—er—machine wasn't in my suitcase, after all."

Viloff's jaw dropped and he stared in open-mouthed amazement.

"No. You see, I thought you might be having a little game, so I took the cork stuffing out of one half of my life-belt and put the machine in instead." He tapped the belt, which he still wore, and at one point it gave out a ring of metal. "It's lucky I didn't fall overboard," he added as he turned away, "or I should have sunk."

* * * *

The next day, Jimmie sitting casually by appointment in St. James' Park, received a large sum in cash for his services in returning the Murchison and in breaking up the most clever and dangerous gang of spies that had troubled the Secret Service for some years. Of this he passed on a large share to Hyslop, which the young man seemed reluctant to take, thanking Jimmie for what he termed "an opportunity to see life" and offering his services if help was wanted in the future for any further undertaking.

Later that afternoon, Jimmie Rezaire gave Vivienne a wad of notes, and took her out to choose frock after frock at the most expensive shops.

"Only look here, Viv," he added in a whisper, "for God's sake don't forget you've now got plenty of money; or we'll be in trouble again. *Do* remember to *pay* when you go!"

www.ingramcontent.com/pod-product-compliance
Lightning Source LLC
Chambersburg PA
CBHW050756250626
47155CB00005B/2096